HEARTLESS GOON 3

Ghost

Lock Down Publications and Ca$h Presents

HEARTLESS GOON 3
A Novel by *GHOST*

Lock Down Publications
P.O. Box 870494
Mesquite, Tx 75187

Visit our website @
www.lockdownpublications.com

Copyright 2019 by Ghost
Heartless Goon 3

First Edition December 2019
Printed in the United States of America

This is a work of fiction. Names, characters, places, and incidents either are products of the author's imagination or are used fictitiously. Any similarity to actual events or locales or persons, living or dead, is entirely coincidental.

Lock Down Publications
Like our page on Facebook: Lock Down Publications @
www.facebook.com/lockdownpublications.ldp
Cover design and layout by: **Dynasty Cover Me**
Book interior design by: **Shawn Walker**
Edited by: **Lashonda Johnson**

Stay Connected with Us!

Text **LOCKDOWN** to 22828 to stay up-to-date with new releases, sneak peaks, contests and more…

Thank you.

Submission Guideline.

Submit the first three chapters of your completed manuscript to ldpsubmissions@gmail.com, subject line: Your book's title. The manuscript must be in a .doc file and sent as an attachment. Document should be in Times New Roman, double spaced and in size 12 font. Also, provide your synopsis and full contact information. If sending multiple submissions, they must each be in a separate email.

Have a story but no way to send it electronically? You can still submit to LDP/Ca$h Presents. Send in the first three chapters, written or typed, of your completed manuscript to:

LDP: Submissions Dept
Po Box 870494
Mesquite, Tx 75187

DO NOT send original manuscript. Must be a duplicate.

Provide your synopsis and a cover letter containing your full contact information.

Thanks for considering LDP and Ca$h Presents.

Dedications:

First of all, this book is dedicated to my Baby Girl 3/10, the love of my life and purpose for everything I do. As long as I'm alive, you'll never want nor NEED for anything. We done went from flipping birds to flipping books. The best is yet to come.

To LDP'S CEO- Ca$h & COO- Shawn:

I would like to thank y'all for this opportunity. The wisdom, motivation, and encouragement that I've received from you two is greatly appreciated.

The grind is real. The loyalty in this family is real. I'm riding with LDP 'til the wheels fall off.

THE GAME IS OURS !

Ghost

Chapter 1

"Let's cause some pain," Grizzly advised.

As soon as he said these words, a text came through on my phone from Veronica. I read over the screen, before Grizzly knocked it out of my hand, and placed his barrel to my Adam's Apple.

Veronica: *Baby, she's dead! Get home now!*

The phone fell to the floor and cracked. It flipped on to its back, all I could see was a zig-zag going down the middle of it. The text kept on replaying through my mind over and over. Who was dead? She coulda meant anybody. Was Veronica talking about my lil' cousin Danyelle, whom I had not spoken to ever since we came under attack by Grizzly, and his goons? Maybe she was talking about, Tamia. The last time I'd seen the mother of my child to be, she was stuck behind the wheel of her truck, after crashing into a parked car while we were under gunfire.

The same gunfire that had sent me and Bubbie in retreat. Bubbie was currently pregnant with my child as well. She was also Tamia's fiercest rival. How I'd gotten both females pregnant at the same time was a long story. Or could she have been talking about my sister, Jahliya? The thought of anything like that happening to her almost made me so weak, I couldn't even stand up straight? Jahliya had been taken by Mikey the head of the Duffle Bag Cartel a few weeks back.

He was demanding a million dollars for her safe return. A million dollars that he expected me to pay in installments of a hundred thousand dollars a week. Payments I'd been making on time. I was praying that she wasn't talking about, Jahliya. I didn't think I was strong enough to endure that.

Grizzly, grabbed me by the throat and placed his Glock to my forehead. "Oh, pussy ass nigga, you done fucked up and got involved with this fuck nigga on that bed, right there? Now you in the same boat. Where the fuck is my money, dope, and diamonds?"

"*Diamonds*?" I didn't know what the fuck he was talking about.

Grizzly mugged Getty. "Oh, so you must not have told him about the diamonds you stole from me?"

Getty refused to look in my direction. He tried to pry himself free of Grizzly's henchmen. "Get the fuck off me. I don't know what you even talking about," he swore, trying his best to break free.

The Asian nurse pulled a syringe out of her black bag. She took the top off it, and popped the side of it, before ordering one of Grizzly's men to hold Getty's left arm out. He followed her orders without so much uttering a word. She looked over her shoulder at Grizzly. "Homeboy already paralyzed from the waist down so he ain't no threat. However, this here gon' stop him from screaming out in pain. Lil' Daddy ain't gon' be able to move a muscle. He only gon' be able to speak loud enough to tell us where my father's diamonds are. Oh, and don't worry, this numbs nothing, he will feel everything." She smiled and jammed the needle into Getty's arm, before pushing down on the dropper.

Getty sat all the way up groaning, then his eyes rolled into the back of his head. "Uh, shit, you muthafuckas," he hissed.

Grizzly tightened his grip around my neck. It wasn't tight enough to choke me, but tight enough to let me know he meant business. I wanted to make a move on him but one of his guards had his silenced gun pinned directly on me.

"You finna watch yo' homeboy get the bidness. Then you gon feel some of this shit before we get a clear understanding. You got that fuck, nigga?" He jammed his gun into my forehead so hard I could feel the breaking of my skin. A trickle of blood ran down the side of my face. The feeling of it only infuriated me. "You hear me, nigga?" He pressed me back into the wall again.

I held my silence. Mentally I was imagining smoking his punk ass. He was treating me like a lame. Like I was soft, or like I really wasn't about that life, when deep down I knew I was pure killa. There was no way I would let him get away with what he'd done to both me and Getty.

The Asian chick smacked Getty as hard as she could and waited for him to holler out in pain. When he gave her a muffled groan, she smiled wickedly and dug back into her bag. This time when she came out, she was holding a pair of pliers in her hand.

"Do you have any idea what they do to you when you steal something in China?" she asked, clamping the Pliers on to Getty's finger and closing it best she could with the jaws of the tool pressing down on his digit.

Getty closed his eyes, opened his mouth and screamed loud as he could, but it sounded as if he was making barely any noise at all. Instead, drool came from his mouth, while the Asian chick, pulled and twisted at his finger until it was all mangled, and barely attached to his hand.

I didn't know what would give them the impression that they could pull off some bullshit like this in a well-known hospital? I expected the police to be making their entrance at any moment. That both scared and gave me a sense of hope. I was scared because, I knew I had taken part in multiple murders, and feared if the cops did run inside the hospital room they would both rescue and prosecute me for what I'd done. If that was going to be the case, I preferred that Grizzly killed me and got it over with.

The Asian chick pulled and stretched his finger from the skin, causing it to tear, and bleed. Then she grabbed a hold of his mouth, digging her fingers into the side of it. "Where are the items you stole from, Grizzly? You are already running out of chances to tell me," she spat and some of her saliva landed directly on Getty's face.

Chapter 2

Getty closed his eyes until she was done asking her question, then he slowly opened them. He looked directly into her face, hawked, and spit the yellowest loogey I'd ever seen. It smacked into her jaw and dripped off her chin, before dripping to the floor. It looked so gross Grizzly turned his head and closed his eyes. I kept watching. I was too heated to be grossed out, although that shit did look nasty.

The Asian chick slowly wiped his spit off her and rubbed it on to his sheets. It left a long streak that looked like egg yolk. She gagged and turned her head away. Seconds later she was back mugging him. "You, sick son of a bitch. Is that how you want to play, things?" She motioned for Grizzly's men to take hold of his hands again. Then she grabbed the same finger with the Pliers and pulled with what seemed like all her might. She twisted and yanked, I couldn't help but notice her grunts, and groans.

Getty looked like he was in excruciating pain. He closed his eyes, while his face began to take upon a series of trans-formations. I felt sorry for my Potna. I didn't know what type of shit he'd gotten us involved in and at that moment I didn't care. I just wanted these muthafuckas to get their shit back so we could go on with our lives. I knew we would find a way to get them back and make them pay.

The Asian, bitch twisted his finger all the way around like a Merry Go Round, then yanked some more. When she fin-ished his finger lay against the back of his hand like a broke cigar. I could see a bone sticking out of the side of it. She slammed his hand against his stomach and took a step back to admire her handy work.

"Getty, I'm going to ask you again. Where are my father's things? This is your last chance to tell me." She picked back up her bag and began to rummage through it. "JaMichael, if I were you, I'd talk some sense into him. If he doesn't return what was taken, he's going to pay, then you will also. Count on that." She pulled a pair of garden shears out of her bag. They looked sharp and shiny.

Getty looked over at me with sweat pouring down his face. "JaMichael, I ain't giving this bitch, or that fuck nigga, shit. I'm just letting you know that, right now. I got plans for that shit. I gotta leave my shawties somethin'. You feel me? That's all they—"

Bam! The Asian punched him in the mouth so hard she knocked him cleanout. Her small fist wound up inside of his mouth. She pulled it back and frowned.

Grizzly stood and laughed like a maniac. "That's how you do a ma'fucka, Shawty? You wait until they get to talking that talk, then punch them right in their shit. Yin put his ass to sleep."

Yin, finally I had a name to go with the person. Yin's fist was bleeding, but she didn't appear to care. She wiped the blood on Getty's forehead and took a hold of his right hand. Then she placed two of his fingers directly into the vee of the blades, and brought them together, cutting off Getty's fingers immediately. He woke up hollering as loud as he could again, but still, it sounded as if he were whispering. I watched his blood spurt out of each socket, then it was dropping down the back of his hand.

Grizzly released me and snapped his fingers at two of his guards. They came and stood in front of me with guns aimed at my face. "If this bitch ass nigga moves, heat his ass up like a shish kabob." He stepped past me and went over to stand beside Getty, looking down on him. "Nigga, how much do you love your daughter, Angel?"

Getty clenched his teeth, more sweat dripped off his chin, as blood continued to pour from his fingers sockets as if they were an open bottle of ketchup. "I'ma kill both of you mutha-fuckas. You, and this punk ass bitch. Mark my words. Y'all gon' get y'alls."

Yin stepped forward and grabbed his cheek with the Pliers. "That's not an answer."

Getty's eyes got as big as a Ferris wheel. "I love my muthafuckin' daughter. This shit ain't got nothin' to do wit' her. This is between me, Grizzly, and Mikey bitch ass."

I was still confused. How did all three parties tie into one another? What the fuck did Getty have us in the middle of? What did he mean by Jahliya's kidnapping had to do with our father Taurus? Who did he kill that was supposed to be close to Mikey? How did Getty connect himself to all of this without telling me?

Grizzly took a hammer from Yin's bag. "Well, it looks like you're on your own, JaMichael. Yo' Potna here fucked you in the game." He twisted the hammer around so that it showed the extractors, and raised it over his head, ready to bring it down on Getty's face.

I could see the anger in his eyes, he'd already made his mind up. "Wait!" I hollered and almost ran over to stop him.

Grizzly's Goons snatched me back up, both of them slammed their guns into the side of my neck. Grizzly laughed and waited before he gave them the signal to hold fast. When he finally did, they took a step back but kept their weapons pinned on me.

"Fuck you gotta say, JaMichael? This nigga time done expired."

"Bruh, hold up. I know the homie will tell me where y'all shit at. Just give me a few minutes to holla at him," I pleaded.

Ghost

Yin stepped forward and punched Getty so hard again that she knocked blood from his mouth. He spit it across his pillow. She grabbed his throat. "Ain't nobody got time to be playing games wit' him. If he wanna go there, we finna go there." She backhanded him, and spit in his face.

Getty laid back against his pillow helpless. I felt like shit for allowing all of that to happen, but I knew honestly there was nothing I could do at that moment. Grizzly and his crew had the ups on both me and Getty. One false move and I knew we'd both be dead. "Fuck these people, JaMichael. They gon' have to kill me. Bury me a muthafuckin' animal. That's how that's finna go."

"What about, Angel? Nigga, you finna let these ma'fuckas kill her, over what?"

Getty was quiet, he spit blood on the floor, and got stuck facing it. I don't know if the drug Yin injected him with had taken its effect or not, but the homie looked fucked up. "They gon' kill me, anyway. I ain't finna give them what the fuck they want, and they get off on me by killing my Shawty. Fuck that, JaMichael. They can kiss my ass." A lone tear streamed down his face. He didn't even bother to wipe it away. "I'm sorry, man. I fucked us over, I did this. I'm sorry, JaMichael." He closed his eyes and laid back. "Kill me, I ain't finna tell you bitches shit."

"Tamia, man!" I yelled, feeling hysterical.

"What?" Getty asked, with his eyes still closed.

"Tamia, she's pregnant with my seed, Getty. Don't make my baby pay for your sins. We're supposed to be better men than that."

Getty opened his eyes and allowed tears to drip. "They gon' kill our people anyway, JaMichael. That nigga Grizzly is shiesty, and so is this Asian bitch, right here. If we give these muthafuckas what they want, they ain't gon' do shit but make

16

a mockery out of me. Now, this shit is all I got put up for my family, and yours, nigga. So, if you wanna tell these ma'fuckas where everything is, be my guest. But I'm telling you, right now that I don't trust them."

Grizzly scoffed and stepped to the side of me. "Nigga, I ain't got shit against you. My beef is with that fuck nigga, right there. All I want is my shit back and you can have yo' peoples, and his, too. That's my word as a man. Tell yo' homie to give you the location of where my shit at, and we good once I get it back."

I looked down at Getty. "Tamia, bruh, Tamia, and Angel. We can't let them go out like this. You already know we can't," I said, feeling my stomach do somersaults.

"A'ight then." Getty forced himself to flip on to his back. "Y'all get the fuck out of the room so I can tell my nigga what's really good. Y'all don't leave then you gon' for sure lose all of that dope and them diamonds. Now get the fuck out!"

Yin waved him off. "You're out of your mind. What the fuck do we look like? You think we're stupid or something?"

"Den fuck you, bitch! I hope yo' daddy kick the moo shoo pork out of yo' ass," Getty snapped, sounding more racist than Donald Trump.

She came out of her inside jacket pocket with a blade and made her way toward him. Grizzly stepped in her path and held up a hand. "Wait a minute, Yin." He took a deep breath and lowered his head.

She frowned and looked him up and down. Her face had turned the color of red. "I'm tired of playin' wit' this ass hole. We can kill him and find the diamonds later. He's not that smart. They can't be hidden that well." She looked past Grizzly, directly into Getty's eyes, and smiled evilly. "I wanna slice yo' bitch ass up and serve you in our restaurant since you think you be talking so slick." She went from smiling to eyeing him with hatred.

Grizzly shook his head. "Nall, fuck that. Time is money. We're on the twelfth floor. We gon' be standing right outside the room. Where the fuck is, they gon' go? After all, Getty bitch ass is paralyzed." He snickered and pulled her closer to him possessively.

She pushed him off and fixed her hair, with blazing speed she placed the blade to my neck, and slowly slid it along my jugular until a trickle of blood oozed into my shirt. "You find out where my father's things are. Or I swear to Buddha, I'll cut your kid out of that bitch myself and throw it out of the window. Then, I'll find you and come kill you. I promise this, JaMichael. Test me if you want to. The Duffle Bag Cartel ain't got shit on the Triad." She licked my cheek, backed away from me and headed to the door of the hospital room. "I'll be out here. The staff was ordered to evacuate this portion of the wing only for another thirty minutes, so chop-chop."

Grizzly stepped to me and rested his hand on my shoulder. "Get the information from your homie, JaMichael. If you don't, then after we stank Tamia. We coming for, Bubbie, Veronica, and Danyelle. I think the Cartel already took care of Jahliya." He clicked his tongue against his teeth and shook his head, before standing in the doorway of the hallway. "Damn, I heard she was bad, too. Y'all got five minutes," He boomed and closed the door.

I was feeling sick from his statements about Jahliya, but I was trying best as I could to not mentally feed into his words. I waited for the door to close before I turned to Getty.

He was laying on his back with tears rolling down the side of his face. "I fucked up, JaMichael. It's because of me that we are about to lose our people." He swallowed his spit and sniffled.

18

"What the fuck are you talking about, Getty? How did you fuck up?"

He shook his head. "Man, I trusted that bitch, Katey. If she is as foul as you're saying she is, then we got a problem."

"Getty, that bitch is dead. How the fuck we gon' have a problem if that bitch ain't even breathing no more?"

"She was supposed to off them diamonds, JaMichael. She had one of the big homies on deck from Chicago. Some major nigga named, Hood Rich."

"What the fuck are you saying? Explain that shit in plain language?"

"Nigga, Katey is the only person that knows I kept the diamonds in my mother's urn inside of her Attic. Nigga, them bitches are worth damn near three million dollars, and if she burned me on the dope. I'm more than sure she burned me on the diamonds, too." He blinked and more tears fell.

"Nigga, how the fuck you gon' hit a three-million-dollar lick, and not include me? I thought we were supposed to be out the mud together?" I felt a lil' hurt and ready to steal his ass because of the betrayal I was feeling.

"Nigga, I thought I had this shit under wraps. Once I got right, I was gon' get you right. It turns out I was fucking with a low life bitch, from the get-go. That's fucked up, ain't it?"

I couldn't do nothing but sigh. "Is there any chance that this bitch didn't get a hold of those diamonds? I mean maybe she was trying to be greedy. Maybe she wanted to knock the both of us off first before she did anything with that nigga, Hood Rich. That way she wouldn't have to rush or nothing like that."

"I don't know what the ho did, but I guess it's worth a shot at trying to find out. Inside of my mother's attic in North Memphis, there is a small trap door right in the back. If you push on this trap door, at the same time twisting the knob upward, it's going to open. When it opens, you'll see a small safe, inside of the safe will be a golden urn. Those are my mother's ashes inside of that urn. The diamonds are inside of her ashes. They were strategically placed all the way at the bottom.

"Nigga, you defiled your mother ashes for some material, shit? What the fuck is wrong with chu?"

"Don't judge me, nigga. That Rebirth had a nigga tripping."

The Rebirth was a powerful form of raw that allowed the fiends to become addicted to the product. It was so bad the drug wound up taking over their lives. I didn't even know Getty was messing around with it on that level but seeing as he had so many secrets, it's no wonder why I didn't know.

"Man, I didn't know yo' ass was as tricky as you are, but it is what it is. I'ma figure out this situation and bring home Angel, and Tamia before these animals fuck them over."

There were two knocks on the door. Yin stepped in the room, followed by Grizzly and his goons. After the last man stepped into the room, he closed the door.

Yin walked up to me and stood in my face. "So?"

"Yeah, bitch, I told him where everything was. I hope he don't give you shit. Tell your father he can kiss my ass and go fu—"

Yin sidestepped, and with unimaginable quickness, pulled the blade from her inside jacket pocket again, before grabbing Getty by the head, and slowly bringing her blade across his neck. She ran the razor's edge across the same incision twice and dropped his head to the pillow. Blood seeped out of his throat and stained the white pillow.

I took a step back in disbelief. I could hear Getty gurgling on his own blood. His eyes remained wide open. He clenched the sheets on each side of him and released his bowels. Yin looked down on him with a sinister frown on her face. She wiped the blade of blood on his sheets and replaced it inside of her small jacket. "Now, JaMichael, take me to my father's stones. If you do this you can keep the heroin and walk away with the girls. I have no use for them, neither does Grizzly."

I continued to watch Getty bleed to death until his eyes rolled back, and he passed away. "Before I do any mutha-fuckin' thang I wanna see, Tamia and Angel. Matter fact, I want them under my care, then you can have yo' precious di-amonds. They ain't got shit to do with me."

Grizzly stepped forward beside me. He pulled the sheet over Getty's face and sighed as if he felt a sense of sympathy for him, although I knew that was the furthest thing from the truth. "JaMichael, just get us our shit, and you can have your people. It's as simple as that."

I stepped in his face. "Listen, Grizzly, you give me them girls, and I'll give you your shit. Everybody can walk away with what belongs to them. If we can't get no understanding, then we can't get no understanding. Y'all can slice my neck too, and you'll be out of more than three million dollars. Now you gotta ask yourself, is that really worth it?"

Yin scrunched her face and balled both fists. "When does this shit end?"

Ghost

Chapter 3

It was a dark and gloomy night. The wind howled from East to West. It smelled like the rain was sure to be on its way real soon. Even with the impending shower looming, there was still an uncomfortable humidity that took over the atmosphere. Grizzly led Tamia to the van by grabbing a handful of her hair and holding her by the back of her shirt. Her mouth and wrists were duct-taped together. He made sure he purposely yanked her head back directly in front of me before he brutally forced her inside the van. She fell beside me with tears running out of her eyes. Her hair looked disheveled. Her clothes were wrinkled, and her stockings were ripped. She looked like she'd been through hell. Angel was already inside the car, and she looked just as bad, it was ridiculous.

Grizzly pulled me out and placed his gun to the back of my head. "A'ight lil' nigga, let's go."

Yin stood with a mask covering half of her face. Her arms were crossed, and she looked like she was over the entire scene already. "Hurry up so we can be done with this trash. We have bigger and better things to be doing than screwing around with this son of a bitch, right here." She turned up her nose and looked off, before opening the driver's door. "I'll be in the van." She climbed inside and slammed it.

Grizzly pressed the gun to the back of my head harder. "Let's go, JaMichael, take me to the diamonds. I ain't got all fucking day," he growled these words through clenched teeth.

I held my hands at shoulder length. "A'ight Potna, damn, chill yo' ass out. You gave me mine, now I'm finna make sure you get yours. I wouldn't know what the fuck to do with those diamonds, anyway." I continued to walk toward the house.

Thanks to one of Grizzly's henchmen the door had been kicked in already and the house had been ransacked from what

I could hear from the report that one of Grizzly's men had told him. But they had come up empty. I was praying I didn't as well. Getty had placed all his trust in Katey. In my opinion, she had been as dirty as they came. So, to say, I wasn't sweating bullets, and paranoid about the outcome I could potentially face would have been a bald-faced lie. I was petrified for the sake of Tamia, my unborn child, and Angel. We had a lot riding on those diamonds, and none of it had to do with money.

When we got inside the house Grizzly grabbed me by the neck from behind and choked me a lil' bit. At the same time, he had his gun pressed to my temple. "Bitch ass nigga if it wasn't for that Asian ho out there, I'd blow yo' brains out. Do you know what yo' punk ass father did to my old man?"

I was stunned, I struggled against him a lil' bit, and gagged, as his arm pulled tighter around my neck. "Let me go," I managed to muster.

He pulled back as hard as he could, then pushed me in the back with force. I fell forward on to the steps and caught myself before my face crashed into the stairs. "Pussy muthafucka, you look just like yo' ugly ass daddy."

I wiped my mouth and eyed him, before coming to my feet. "What the fuck is yo' problem, Grizzly? We came in here for one reason. That's to get yo' shit back, that's all. I don't wanna hear nothin' about what my Pops did. That shit ain't got nothing to do wit' me."

Grizzly mugged me for a moment, then he was motioning for me to stand up straight. Once I was, he aimed his gun at my forehead. This was the first time I noticed that he had a silencer on the end of his weapon. "You ever heard of a legend in Memphis named, Jerry Walker?"

I nodded. "Yeah, Jerry Walker was one of the first kingpins in Memphis history to make a million dollars way back in the day. What about him?"

Grizzly clenched his teeth. "Well, yo' punk ass father, Taurus and your uncle Juice ran into Jerry Walker's after hour spot and murdered my father in cold blood. After they murdered him my mother took to heroin and overdosed a month later. My sister got hooked on that shit as well. Your father fucked over my family. Nigga this shit is way deeper than some fuckin' diamonds. This here is about blood and retribution."

I didn't give a fuck what my father had done to his family. Clearly, all that shit had taken place before I was even alive. "Like I said before, that shit ain't got nothin' to do with me. Now let's get these diamonds and everybody can leave this bitch happy, and free!" I sidestepped him and punched him as hard as I could right in the jaw, I hit his ass super hard.

He stumbled back, raised the gun and shot twice, because of the way his arm was positioned he wound up putting two slugs in the ceiling of Getty's mother's house. I tackled him like a linebacker on steroids. He crashed into the wall and dropped the gun. As soon as he did, I wiggled out of his grasp and kicked it across the floor. It wound up about ten feet away from us. I made my way to pick it up. I had every intention of grabbing it and unloading the full clip on his ass. Then I was going to go outside and do the same to Yin. That sick bitch had killed my right-hand man, she had to pay.

Before I could reach the gun Grizzly's big ass was up and jumping on my back. It felt like a car had fallen out of the sky and landed on me. We fell to the ground, and I heard my bones crunch from the weight of his fat ass. The next thing I knew he was sitting on me and raining down blows to the back of my head. Them sons of bitches hurt, too. I musta received about twenty blows, before I hollered, and with all my might, raised up and threw his big ass off me. I came to my feet, and he charged at me swinging wildly.

As soon as he got within arms-length I dropped to the ground, and punched him square in the nuts, then brought my head up, and bust his face wide open. Blood spilled out of it immediately, but he kept on coming like a maniac in a horror movie. The blood rushed into his eyes and made it hard for him to see. He kept on trying to wipe it out. My fist caught him in the right eye, busting it, then the left. His head snapped back. I was on his ass, rushing at full speed. I picked him up in the air and slammed him directly on the stairs. He let out a yelp, then my Jordan's were stomping his face as if I'd seen a whole bunch of roaches crawling around on it, I went crazy. Thank God, he'd made his security stay outside along with Yin, and my girls.

Grizzly continued to take my assault until he passed out in a mess of his own blood. Even then, I kept on stomping and crushing his bones. After a while, his structure felt like mush. He was no longer moving, he laid straight out. His face looked swollen and broken. I rested against the wall while I caught my breath. My chest felt like there was an elephant sitting on it. My lungs burned, and I didn't know what to do next. I picked up his silenced .45, cocked it, jogged to the back of the house to see if I could still see the van that we'd rolled in parked in the back alley. I could, but just the front end of it, and that was enough for me.

I rushed back inside to make sure Grizzly still lay dead on the floor. He did, I grabbed his ankles, and pulled him into the pantry that was connected to the kitchen. Once he was inside of there, I closed the pantry door. Then I was climbing the stairs and making my way to the attic. The hallway felt humid and sticky. The stairs creaked and there was no railing. I felt a major sense of anxiety the higher I climbed. I knew I was on the clock. Yin would only allow us to be inside for so long before she started to suspect something wasn't right. I had to hurry. There was no way around it. I was just praying Katey hadn't gotten to the stash before I'd had the chance too.

I followed all the directions that Getty had given me. When I got to the safe, I punched in his mother's birthday just like he'd given me. The safe took a few extra seconds before it hissed and popped open. As soon as it did, I reached inside and pulled out the urn containing Getty's mother's ashes. My heart beat faster than a sprinter on the pavement in a race. I kneeled and poured her ashes on the ground. I felt sorry for doing it, but what had to be done had to be done. It felt like it took a million years for me to dump out half of them. The dust from her remains billowed into the air and got into both my eyes and mouth. I spit and tried to not freak out about the fact that I had corpse remains on my tongue.

When seventy-five percent of the ashes were dumped out, I started to panic, wondering if Getty had sent me off. He was full of so many secrets, maybe he had chosen to take one more to his grave. I was already cursing him out in my head when the first sparkly diamond appeared. A second later, then another, and another. Finally, I was pouring them into a pile in front of me. I got so happy I was forgetting to breathe. I was starting to scoop them one by one back into the urn when there was the sound of a gun cocking back. Then I felt cold steel pressed to between my left ear lobe, and my head. I dropped everything and held my hands up.

Yin laughed. "So, I see you took advantage of a weak, Grizzly." She clicked her tongue against her teeth three times. "Such a pity for that fool. Are those my diamonds?"

I nodded. "Yeah, and a deal is a deal. I got yo' shit, now you gotta let me have my people back so we can get on with our lives."

"Put them back into that fancy canister you got, right there. Hurry up," she ordered, hitting me on top of the head to let me know that she meant bidness. "And place your gun on the floor. Do it!"

I slowly set the .45 on the ground, but close enough that I could get to it if I saw the opportunity to do so. Then I was taking the diamonds and placing them back into Getty's mother's urn. "Yin, don't be on that bullshit, Shawty. I don' did everything I was supposed to do. Now you gotta hold up your end."

"Shut up, just keep loading up that thing with my father's stones. You aren't running the show, I am." She extended her arm and aimed her gun again. "Don't make me remind you of that again."

"Alright, alright, look I only got a few more, see?" I continued to load up the canister. When I got down to the last one, I stood up and placed it inside the urn. I put the lid back on it and twisted the top. "Here you go, a deal is a deal."

She adjusted the gun in her hand, then reached to take a hold of the urn. "You have no idea how much havoc you have just saved yourself."

Bocka! Bocka! Bocka! Bocka!

Yin turned her head to look out of the window. Taking advantage of the distraction, I cocked back and brought my fist forward, it crashed directly into her chin and knocked her cleanout. The gun slid across the ground. The urn fell, and rolled to the wall, and stopped. I picked it up, along with her .9 millimeter. When I looked over my shoulder to see if she was even trying to get up, I saw that she was out like a light.

Bocka! Bocka! Bocka! Bocka!

Screaming ensued from the back of the house. The first person I thought about was Tamia. I just knew somebody had done something to her. I figured it was Mikey's bitch ass. My stomach turned over three times. I kept seeing the text that Veronica had sent me about somebody being dead, then I started imagining both Jahliya, and Tamia in a casket. The image was enough to drive me nearly insane.

Bocka! Bocka! Bocka! Bocka!

I ran down the back stairs, when I got to the back door of the house thunder roared in the sky. A few seconds later, it was pouring down hard. I pulled the door open and ran out into the night. The heavy scent of gunpowder and blood flooded my nostrils. Rain attacked my face and I became instantly cold. It was pitch black out except the lightning that came every few seconds and illuminated the sky. After a quick jolt, it was gone, and the night became as black as a blank piece of black construction paper. The only consistent lighting came from the alley that was no more than twenty yards away from me. I began running as fast as I could. When I finally made it there what I saw blew my mind.

Ghost

Chapter 4

Chino held Tamia in his arms and carried her to his Hummer, as the rain beat down on both of them. Behind him were two dead bodies laid on the pavement, both heavily riddled with bullets. Chino's men were masked up like Freddie Krueger. They held fully automatic weapons in their hands. One of the riffles were still smoking. To the left of them were two men hanging out the side door of the van that I'd been in. Both men's heads were half blown off. The rain assaulted the bloody concrete under the vehicles.

Chino aimed his gun at me, and a red beam appeared from the top of it. The laser rested on my forehead. "Is that you, JaMichael?" he hollered.

I held my hands up. "Yeah, nigga, it's me! Where the fuck is, Tamia?"

He pointed toward his Hummer. "She good, and she's wit' me for now." Sirens sounded in the background. "Don't worry about her, JaMichael, I got her." He backed up, and rushed to his Hummer, then jumped inside. He waited for his men to get in, then they were speeding away down the alley.

"Wait!" I chased the Hummer for a minute and stopped halfway. I stood there looking stupid. When I turned around to walk back to the van, that's when I saw Angel coming down the alley covered in blood.

She cried and reached her arms out for me. "Uncle!"

***

Bubbie came out of the bathroom carrying Angel wrapped in a towel. She placed her on the couch and kissed her on the forehead. "There you go, Princess. You just sit here and play with this iPad while I talk to your Uncle. We'll be back in a few minutes," she said, looking down at Angel with what appeared to be genuine concern. Bubbie came, took a hold of my hand and led me to the guest bedroom where she had Angel all set up to sleep for the night. "Baby, explain what happened to tonight."

"Bubbie I can't even think straight until Veronica returns this text, and tells me who she's talking about, that's supposed to be dead. If it turns out to be, Jahliya, I'm about to lose my fuckin' mind." I sat on the edge of the bed and rubbed my hands over my face.

I was stressing like never before, I couldn't even think straight. Not only was I worried about my sister, but the whole thing that took place with Tamia was blowing my mind. Chino, nor Tamia were answering their phone. That only made me fear the worst.

Bubbie stepped in front of me and held my face in her little hands. She directed me to look up at her. "Daddy, I need you to know that you are not alone. We are in this together. If you need me to handle anything for you, I got your back. I hope you know that." She leaned forward to kiss my lips.

I turned my head and she was only able to plant a peck on my cheek. "Shawty, you said you was finna get my sister back. You said I didn't have to worry about that no more. Yet, here I am stressing. I don't know if my sister is dead or alive. So, don't feed me that you riding wit' me shit, because if you was she'd be sitting right here beside me already." I stood up and bumped her lil' ass out of the way. "Where your phone?"

She pointed toward the dresser. "JaMichael, are you giving up on me?" Her voice sounded a little whiney and for me at that time it was irritating.

"I been gave up. You ain't on shit, because if you was, I'd have my sister back." I sent Veronica another text, then called her phone. It rang and rang with no answer. Her voice mailbox was full. "Damn!" I said, slapping my hands together. I didn't even care that I broke her phone in the process. "Bubbie, if yo' cousin hurt my sister, I'm telling you, right now, I'm finna wipe out your entire bloodline. I ain't finna have no mercy on none of you muthafuckas. I promise you that." I started pacing.

Bubbie stood with her back against her white dresser. Her stomach had a slight bulge to it. Her face appeared fuller and even in my stressed mood, I had to admit she looked good.

"Baby, I don't know what Mikey is doing, but I will say this, I love you. When it all boils down I'm riding with you over anybody else. You're not only our child's father, but you're my man. We are in this shit together." She opened her arms to wrap them around my body for a hug.

I slapped the palm of my hand against her forehead, stopping her. "Man, until Jahliya gets back home safe, I can't trust you, and I can't fuck wit' you on that level. You, steady talking about, you riding for me, man, bitch, please. That shit go in one ear, and out the other. Fuck yo' bloodline, right now. Get the fuck out of my way." I waved her to move to the side.

She sidestepped but before I could get down the hallway good she was on my ass. "You evil son of a bitch, I'm carrying your child, right now. This child is going to have my bloodline as well as yours. Let me tell you a little about my bloodline. We are loyal people. We kill for those we love. Our devotion is second to none. We are Dostiers, you're gon' learn about my bloodline through me real fast."

"Fuck yo' bloodline, I ain't tryna learn shit about yo' people. You tryna make it seem like y'all all high and mighty and shit. That nigga Phoenix is as dirty as they come. He and the majority of them Duffel Bag Cartel niggas. If he dirty, that means you got that snake shit in you, too. You know how that bloodline shit work. And it's like I said before, if that nigga,

Mikey, laid a hand on my sister, I'm coming for him, and that fool Phoenix. I'm wiping out every muthafucka they love and care about over, Jahliya. Now I know, Phoenix is your cousin, so that means a whole lot of your people run the risk of getting caught in the crossfire. To be honest, I don't give no fuck," I said the last part as nasty as I possibly could.

Bubbie stood with her back against the hallway wall. She had her head lowered nodding. "You know what, JaMichael, while we're talking about corrupt bloodlines and shit. Let's talk about yours. I hope you know, your family's business is well known all up and down Memphis. Your father, Taurus was a legend, but that ain't all he was known for. He was also known for fuckin' his own mother. And if he's your father then that must mean that same sick shit is inside of you," she spat. "What you got to say about that?"

I stepped into her face and pressed my forehead against hers. She stood on her tippy toes and tried as hard as she could to push my head back. "Shawty, I don't give a fuck what you say about me, but leave my pops, my mother, and Jahliya out of your mouth or I'm gon' be forced to pop yo' ass in that ma'fucka. You understand me?"

She sucked her teeth and looked into my eyes. "You think I'm scared of you, JaMichael? Well, if you do let me be the first to tell you, I ain't afraid of you. I might be a female, but I got more heart than most of them niggas out there walking around. You gon' learn that shit real fast."

"Like I said, keep my people out yo' mouth, and we'll be good." I walked into the living room and grabbed my jacket. I was getting ready to snatch up Angel so we could go to a hotel for the night until I figured out where we were going to be for the long haul when Bubbie walked into the living room and grabbed my wrist aggressively.

I yanked it away from her, at the same time her phone buzzed with a text from Veronica.

Veronica: *JaMichael, have you seen Danyelle. Do you know where she's at?*

JaMichael: *Where are you, Auntie? Who did you say was dead? And no, I haven't seen, Danyelle. I don't know where she's at.*

Bubbie stepped around into my face again. "Why is it okay for you to talk shit about what you're going to do to my people if Mikey laid a finger on your sister? But when I say one little thing about Taurus you get ready to abuse me? What type of shit is that?" she snapped blocking my path.

I tried to step around her again, but once again she was there just like an annoying ass bug, getting on my fuckin' nerves. Finally, I picked her up and carried her back into her room, tossing her on the bed. Angel had been in the living room playing away on the iPad that Bubbie supplied her with. I didn't want to disturb her with our argument, so I thought it would be better if I took Bubbie back into her bedroom, so we could get a clear understanding.

She bounced off the bed and looked pissed. "Why the fuck did you bring me in here?"

I grabbed her by the throat and held her against the wall. "Listen to me and listen good, Bubbie. I'ma need you to stop playin' wit' me and stop testing me like I'm one of these average Memphis niggas. On my mother in heaven, I'll beat yo' lil' ass like you my daughter or something."

She scratched at my wrist and wound up with a gang of blood in her nails. I released my hold on her. As soon as my hand dropped, she smacked me so hard I felt my neck pop. "You bitch ass, nigga. Don't you ever put your fuckin' hands on me again." She pushed me with both hands as hard as she could. "I'm tired of your shit, JaMichael. That's not how you're supposed to treat me. I'm pregnant with your fuckin' kid. I demand respect!" She rushed me with her arms swinging in a windmill type fashion.

I blocked blow after blow, slipped under her tenth blow and wound up behind her. I grabbed her and pulled her to my body. "Baby, chill, I'm sorry. Daddy's so so sorry. I didn't mean to choke you out. Forgive me, okay?"

"Let me go, Ghost! Let me go, right now. I'm so tired of you treating me like trash. I'm sick of it." She was crying already and trying her hardest to fight out of my hold.

I turned her around and rested my lips against her forehead. "Daddy, sorry baby. I'm so so, sorry. Please calm down, you done already smacked the shit out of me." My face was still on fire from her smack. The only reason, I ain't tear her ass up is because that beating women shit really ain't in me. I would fuck a nigga up any day of the week but when it came to a female, I felt like dudes that beat on women were nothin' but lowkey bitches, and that bitch shit ain't in me.

Bubbie struggled against me for a little while longer, then her struggles turned into her hugging my waist tightly. "Damn, Daddy, I'm sorry for smacking you, but you had no right putting your hands on me. You gotta catch yourself when you feel like doing that from here on out. Do you hear me?"

I just maintained my silence because I didn't know if I could commit to anything like that. "Baby let's go in here, and get Angel squared away for the night, then I can get you right. Okay?"

She sucked on her bottom lip. "Do you really apologize, though?"

I nodded. "Yeah, boo, I do."

"Then give me a kiss?" She puckered up her lips and closed her eyes.

I leaned forward to kiss her lips. As soon as my skin settled on hers, her phone vibrated with a text.

Veronica: Hey, JaMichael, where are you? Are you sitting down?

I broke my embrace with Bubbie to respond.

JaMichael: *Hey Auntie, I'm at home. Yes, I'm sitting down. What's goin' on?*

"Who is that on my phone?" Bubbie asked, rubbernecking, trying to see what she could see.

"Baby move, I'm doing somethin', right now." I waited for a response from Veronica but nothing. I grew more and more impatient with every minute that passed by. My worry turned to irritation, and I went off.

JaMichael: *Hey Auntie, I'm worried about you. What's goin' on?*

JaMichael: *Auntie? What's up, man? What's wrong?*

JaMichael: *Talk to me. What's goin' on?*

JaMichael: *Hellooo! Don't ignore me.*

JaMichael: *Stop fuckin' playin'! What's up?*

JaMichael: *I'm not about to play these games man, what's up?*

JaMichael: *????*

JaMichael: *Hellooo!*

JaMichael: *Hellooooo!*

JaMichael: *Helloooooo!*

Bubbie stood across the room looking me over, with her arms crossed in front of her chest. When she figured I wasn't going to get a response, she came across the room and sat on my lap. "JaMichael, baby, you need to take it easy. Or you are going to drive yourself crazy. Now, who was that on the phone?"

Instead of answering her, I passed her the phone and allowed her to read the messages herself. When she finished, she took my head and rested it against her shoulder. "Daddy, I'm pretty sure everything is going to be okay. We'll just go to Veronica's first thing in the morning. She'll tell us what's going on, and we'll go from there. Okay?"

I felt like I was losing my mind. All I wanted was Jahliya back. I needed to know she was safe and sound. Even if Mikey still had her, and was demanding a ransom I would accept that, as long as I knew there was breath still inside her body. That's all that mattered to me.

"Yeah, a'ight baby, but make sure you leave your ringer on as loud as it can go. I know Veronica gon' be hitting me back up. I don't know what the fuck is going on with her." I could literally feel my body ready to shut down because I was so tired. I yawned and Bubbie covered my mouth for me.

She kissed my cheek. "Daddy, let's go in here and put Angel to sleep, so we can go to bed. Tomorrow is a new day." She hugged my neck and kissed me on the lips. "I love you so much. I just thought I should let you know that. I promise we're going to get, Jahliya, back. I'm riding wit' you until the death, you'll see." She hugged me tighter. "Now come on."

Chapter 5

About three o'clock in the morning, I woke up to Bubbie straddling my waist. She leaned down and sucked on my neck. "Get up, Daddy. I need some of you, like, right now." She scooted back and trailed her tongue down the middle of my chest. In seconds, she had my dick sticking up out of my boxer hole, stroking it with long pumps. "Get up, Daddy." She kissed the head and sucked it into her mouth, taking me half-way, before pulling me back out.

There was nothing like the feeling of waking up to some good boss. Bubbie was making all kinds of noises around my shit, too. I started moaning deep within my throat and slowly working my dick in and out of her lips. It felt so good. "Damn, baby, what time is it?"

She popped me out and kept stroking me. My dick was nicely lubricated with her spit. "It's time for you to cum in yo' baby's pussy. It feels like it's been forever, Daddy." Then she was back to sucking me like a veteran. Every now and then she would pop my piece out so she could talk shit to me and so she could feel my dick rise longer and longer. "I love you, Daddy." More sucking. "You belong to me." Deepthroating some more. "I'll kill for you, I swear to God I will." She tightened her fist on me and started sucking as if her life depended on it. When her teeth nipped the head, she caused me to shiver, a moment later, I was cumming in her sucking lips.

"Uh-uh-uh, shit, Bubbie!"

She kept right on sucking and swallowing until she couldn't force any more seed out of me. After she finished that, she pulled me on top of her and pushed down on my fore-head. "My turn, Daddy, I want you to taste me."

She opened her thighs as wide as they could go and rubbed her bald pussy. She smushed the lips together, then opened them up so I could see her pink insides. It looked glossy, there was a trail of juice that leaked from her hole to the top of her ass crack.

I took my tongue and licked up the entire trail. I didn't stop until my lips wrapped around her clit. Once there I started sucking on her vagina's nipple as if I had a gun pointed at the back of my head. She tasted both salty and sweet. She wrapped her thighs around my cheeks and humped upward, grunting and groaning.

"Unnhhh, Daddy! Daddy, fuck-unnhhh-unnhhh! Eat me—eat yo', baby. Fuck! Fuck—aww shoooottt!" she screamed and covered her face with a pillow.

Her ankles hung over my shoulders, she sat all the way up and came squirting into my mouth. I felt the jets on my tongue and kept right on licking, and swallowing. The way I saw it was that she was, my baby's mother, and it was my job to enjoy the taste of her pussy and that I did.

After she came, I flipped her on her back and ate that pussy from the back while she beat her fist on the bed. Tears came out of her eyes. She kept cumming and cumming, and I kept swallowing that shit. The louder she moaned the more it turned me on. When she slid to all fours, reached under herself and opened her sex lips, I nearly broke my neck positioning myself behind her, so I could slide home. She helped to guide me in. Then she was pushing back on me, provoking and encouraging me to fuck her harder and harder.

"Harder, Daddy! Uh-uh-uh-uh, harder! Ooo-shit, I—love—it, harder!" She started to growl, grabbing the sheets into her fist, and fucking back into me.

Sweat appeared on the side of her head. It made her baby hairs curl up. The scent of her perfume and pussy was perfectly loud in the room. I held her waist and dogged that ass from the back. Watching my dick go in and out of her drove me crazy. I liked how the contrast looked of my black piece, slicing in and out of her golden-colored sex lips. The lips were swollen, and juicy.

She came hard, and fell on her stomach, with me still pounding her out. I sucked on the back of her neck until I came twice. Then I pulled her on top of me, and we fell asleep just like that. Her pussy continued to ooze our sex juices while we slept. I was thankful that she had woken me up with something on her mind because our fuck session allowed me to think about something else other than my current circumstances, even if it was only for a little while.

***

"Daddy? Daddy, wake up, it's somebody here that wants to talk to you," Bubbie said pushing me awake.

I sat straight up in the bed rubbing my eyes. Then I looked over at the clock that was on her nightstand and saw that it was 12:27 in the afternoon. I felt tired as hell, I closed my eyes back. "Who the fuck wanna talk to me?" I asked, laying back down, I was still barely there consciously. I felt somebody sitting on the bed. That made me open my eyes. When I did, I looked straight into the face of Veronica, my aunt.

There were slight bags under her eyes. She looked like she'd just finished crying. "Ghost, I need to talk to you for a minute."

I sat straight up and rubbed my fists in my eyes to get the cold out. I couldn't believe she was actually there. I was happy to see her, but at the same time, it made me nervous. I felt that she was getting ready to give me some news I couldn't handle. "What's good, Auntie?" I pulled her to me and kissed her on the forehead.

She smiled and sighed. "Baby, I don't know how to say this, so I'm just gon' come right out and say it. I think that Cartel killed, Jahliya."

My heart felt like it stopped for a few seconds. I couldn't breathe, I stood up and dropped the covers from around me. I didn't even care that I was naked, and probably smelling like Bubbie's pussy. I started pacing back and forth like an angry and confused Lion. "Veronica, what would make you say some dumb shit like that?"

She sat still for a minute, then she got up and turned to face me. "I just heard that through the grapevine. One of the sistahs at church was eavesdropping, she was saying that she heard her son talking about that to somebody on the phone. She said that he said, Jahliya's name more than once."

My vision started getting real blurry. I needed to have a seat, but I refused to sit down. "Who the fuck is this, nigga, Veronica? I want his address, right now! Do he work for Mikey and 'nem?"

She shrugged her shoulders. "Baby, I don't know, I wish I did, but I can find out. I can ask the sistah, and she can ask him. It's his mother so I'm pretty sure he would tell her."

I shook my head. "Fuck that, you gon give me Shawty address, and I'm gon investigate this shit myself. Man, if anybody killed my sister, I swear to God it's finna be a whole ass serial killer loose in Memphis. I ain't finna spare nobody." I punched my fist into my hand. "Why the fuck you ain't answer your phone last night? Didn't you see that it was me calling yo' ass?" I snapped, I couldn't help it.

I was way more heated than I honestly realized. I needed to take my frustrations out on somebody. She seemed like the perfect candidate, that was until I could get my hands on, Mikey, and all his bitch ass niggas.

"My battery was on one percent while I was going back and forth with you at first. Then all of a sudden it died. I couldn't find my charger, so this morning I went and bought one. I'm sorry, JaMichael, please don't be mad at me." She lowered her head and looked up at me with sad eyes. "Can you forgive me?"

I sighed and nodded. "Yeah, I can't sweat that shit. I know you ain't do it on purpose." I walked to Bubbie's big window and looked out of it. "Damn, bitch ass niggas!" I was clenching my teeth so hard I could hear them creaking. "Man, if that nigga, Mikey hurt Jahliya, I swear to God." I felt so weak and sick over Jahliya.

"It seems like she been going through this ever since she was young," Veronica said in a hoarse, low voice.

I looked over my shoulder at her. "What are you talking about?"

"When she was little your grandfather and uncle Juice took her away from Taurus. Juice was something like your father's enemy. He tried to kill and hurt him anyway that he could. He also tried to hurt him by kidnapping your sister when she was barely two years old. It's a long story, but the end result was that your father had to tear up the city until he got Jahliya back. Taurus and Princess had to tear some stuff up. Now it's like history is repeating itself only now you're in the driver's seat to get her back. I'd say Lord willing she is still alive, and when you get her back y'all need to just go somewhere where you'll both be safe. It seems like my niece is cursed, or maybe it's just Taurus's bloodline altogether."

"But his bloodline is your bloodline, Veronica."

"I know, and I ain't been able to get in touch with, Danyelle. I don't know where that girl at either, and I'm starting to panic." She came and buried her face in my chest.

I rubbed her back. "It's gon' be okay, Auntie, I got you. While I'm out there looking for, Jahliya, I'll find Danyelle, too. I got you." I hugged her tightly.

Bubbie came into the room and cleared her throat. "Uh, Veronica, your daughter is in the living room crying. I think you should go in there and holla at her. She's freaking out Angel. So, I put her in the other guest bedroom with the iPad, but I don't know how much longer that's going to keep her calm."

Veronica bounced up from the bed and rushed into the living room. "Girl, where the fuck have you been?" Were the last words I heard before Bubbie closed the door.

She rested with her back against it. "Daddy, I got something in the works, right now. I need to know what you are thinking?"

"I'm thinking about killing some shit, Bubbie. Veronica talking about she thinks this nigga done killed my sister. What the fuck am I supposed to be thinking?"

Bubbie came across the room and stood in front of me. "Take me wit' chu."

I mugged her lil' ass. "What are you talking about?"

She looked into my eyes and stepped closer. She placed the palms of her hands on my shoulders and repeated herself. "Daddy, you finna go holla at this nigga who you think got something to do with, Jahliya, right?"

"You damn right I am. He gotta know something about where Mikey's holding my sister."

"Well, I want you to take me with you. I want you to show me how to handle a nigga. That way I can have your back in the way I am supposed to. I also got somebody that wanna holla about those diamonds you got in that knapsack over there." She nodded with her head.

I looked over at the purple Crown Royal bag on the dresser that I had placed the diamonds inside right before I'd given Angel her lunch. "You going through my shit, now?"

She waved me off. "We finna have a kid together. What's yours is mine from here on out. But back to bidness, when you stank this nigga over Jahliya I wanna be there. I also got some spots I want us to hit up. It turns out that Phoenix and Mikey are in straight beef mode. When he gets back from Texas, he's going to help us in finding your sister. But in the meantime, and between times, I wanna ride beside you while you take apart the Duffel Bag Cartel member by member. We are in this together." She stepped on her tippy toes and kissed my lips, with her eyes closed.

I don't know why, but Bubbie was getting to me like never before. I was imagining me handling my bidness while she stood back and watched me do my thing, that excited me. On top of that, I could only imagine how shit would be if I turned her into a savage like me. I think every man that's been in the life would love to have his female ready to body something on the strength of him.

"Baby, you ain't got the slightest idea what I got going through my head, right now. You make it seem like you're down for this shit, and you don't have the slightest idea what you're about to get yourself into."

She shook her head. "I don't care, if it got anything to do with you, I'm riding ten toes down. Fuck those niggas. Let's do what you gotta do. I'ma show you where my loyalties lie and that a girl can be just as much of a killa as a boy can." She crossed her arms and frowned her pretty face.

I couldn't do nothing but laugh at that. I pulled her to me and wrapped my arms around her small frame. "I never thought shit would turn out like this. But I love you for standing by my side, Bubbie, I mean that shit."

She softened. "So, does that mean it's going to make you nicer toward me or—" she joked, but I knew her joke had a hint of seriousness to it.

"Yeah, baby, but just toward you. The rest of the world can feel this pain until I get my sister back." I meant that shit.

I could still hear Veronica and Danyelle arguing in the living room, but my mind was somewhere else. I found myself getting lost with Bubbie being posted in my arms the way that she was.

"We on bidness the first thing in the morning. I kissed her forehead. "What you think about that?"

"It sounds good to me, Daddy. Let's do this, I'm ready to prove my love to you."

Just her carrying my seed alone was enough to make me love and be crazy over her, but the way she was talking had me drowning in her in a way that I never thought was possible. I guess it was easy for niggas to fall for that rough and rugged, 'bout that life type females, too, Bubbie had me gone.

Chapter 6

The next day it was hot and sunny outside. The weather was so humid and muggy that before I climbed into Bubbie's Range Rover my clothes were sticking to me. I sat in her passenger's seat and leaned it all the way back. Veronica had already done her research and found out that the sistah who went to her church son's name was Ralphie. Ralphie was an upcoming hustler inside of the Duffel Bag Cartel. He already had three trap houses and was pushing a 2020 money green Porsche on twenty eights. For a nigga to be rolling something like that in Memphis he had to be plugged and moving some serious weight.

Bubbie pulled the Range Rover into Shante's Chicken and Waffles and found a parking spot right beside Ralphie's Porsche. She kept the engine running and stepped out of the truck with her Burberry denim daisy dukes up in her ass. Both of her caramel cheeks were out and jiggling like crazy. She rocked a pair of Chanel sunglasses before she stepped into the restaurant, she lowered them, and eyed him seductively, then pushed them back up on her nose. She looked so good, she had my dick hard as Calculus.

Ralphie was a heavyset, light-skinned nigga with long, reddish dreads and a pair of Ray-Ban sunglasses on his face. He stood up and peered over the windshield of his truck before jumping out and following Bubbie inside. The parking lot was pretty scarce with the exception of two other cars. The occupants were already inside the restaurant. I took in the whole scene through Bubbie's mirror tints. I could see Ralphie inside seemingly spitting his best game. Bubbie laughed at him and stroked his arm a few times.

This musta made him really feel like he was getting somewhere because when it came time for her to pay for the food,

Ralphie pulled out a dummy knot and bought it for her. Minutes later, he followed her outside and to the truck. They chatted for a moment, then she climbed into the truck. She sat the bag of food on the back seat and slammed the door. I kept my seat leaned all the way back.

"We got his ass, Daddy." She slowly pulled out of the parking space, and lowered her window, looking down on him. "Mane, gon' head, I'ma follow you."

"A'ight, that sound like a plan, baby girl, you fucking wit' the right one."

"Now, I already told you it bet not be nobody else there but you. If I get there and it's anybody else there I'm leaving, and you can lose my number."

"Shawty, dis my suite. Fuck I look like letting somebody else be where I chill, wit' a fine one like ya self? Dat ain't my swag, Shawty, I'm talking big facts."

She nodded. "A'ight then, I guess we rolling, make yo' move."

"Already." He jumped into his Porsche and sped out of his parking spot. He hit three doughnuts in the middle of the parking lot. Smoke rose from his high-priced tires, then he stormed out of the parking lot and jumped on the freeway.

Bubbie laughed. "Dis nigga finna be so sweet that we get cavities. Doing all that flexing shit for what? That Porsche ain't hitting on nothing." She got on to the freeway and followed him.

"Shawty what are you doing?"

"Baby, you wanted to drag that fool somewhere and get information out of him. I'm thinking it'll be smarter if we deal with him in his own habitat." She picked up the cup of pop and handed it to me. "Baby, do me a favor and slide that straw inside this drink for me, I'm thirsty as hell." She used her clicker, and switched lanes, making sure she stayed as close to him as possible. He made me nervous because he was talking on the phone. I wondered who he was talking to, too?

I handed Bubbie back the pop once I slid the straw through the top of it. "Shawty, who the fuck told you to come up with yo' own plan. You supposed to be following me."

She smiled and stuck her tongue out at me. "Daddy, it's like I told you, we are in this together. I know you're cut from the streets and all that, but so am I. I think two heads are much better than one. So, it'll work if you put a plan on the table, and we come up with the best strategy for both of us to succeed. At the end of the day if you fail, then I ultimately fail. So, our shit gotta be on fleek." She kept rolling for a minute.

"I don't like this nigga being on the phone either. That shit's making me paranoid."

I mugged his Porsche and made sure I continued to stay as low as possible in my seat. I had two .40s on my waist, and if I had to, I would empty both magazines with no problem. "I agree wit' you, Boo, but from here on out don't be making no moves without running that shit by me first. I am still the head of this whole damn thang, Shawty, and we can't forget that my sister's life is on the line here."

She reached over and squeezed my thigh. "Okay, that sounds good to me, Daddy. But please just know that I'd never do anything to jeopardize our mission. I wanna make you so happy and show you that you can depend on me more than the streets."

I didn't respond to that, I had visions of clapping Ralphie, and if that was the case I needed to mentally be in straight kill mode. I couldn't be on that sappy shit, even though, deep down Bubbie had me feeling some type of way. She was in my heart already. I know I said that before, but the more killa shit she got on, the more I felt a connection to her.

She looked over at me and smiled weakly, then looked forward, driving. I could tell she wanted to say something but kept rolling. "Look, he's getting off up there, we should be close now."

I nodded, I don't know why but I wanted to tell her lil' ass that I loved her. I refrained because once again, we had to stay on that killa frame of mind.

"Baby, can I ask you a question without you getting all irritated and shit?" she asked, continuing to follow behind Ralphie.

"Do it got anything to do with this lick we finna hit, right now?"

She shook her head. "Nall, but, it's still important."

"Well, if it ain't got nothing to do with what we doing, right now, keep that shit to yourself. Whenever you out here in these streets, bussing a move, you need to be focused on strictly that. We can talk about all that other shit another time. Now shut up and focus. You hear me?"

She frowned. "Yeah, Daddy, I hear you."

We drove in silence for the rest of the way. I didn't like coming down on her so hard, but that's just how shit had to go. I needed her to be a heartless goon when we were out doing our thing. Any false moves could get her and my unborn Shawty iced, and that would murder me.

***

An hour later, I found myself waiting under the bathroom window of Ralphie's crib. I was cursing Bubbie out under my breath and wondering what the fuck was taking her so long. Apart of me begin to panic, I was also on some sucka shit, hoping she wasn't inside actually fuckin' this nigga. I imagined his piece running in and out of my baby mother's body, bussing all on my Shawty's forming head, and that got me heated. I was about to say fuck it and climb inside of his crib the best way I knew how, when Bubbie opened the bathroom window, and stuck her head out. She looked right, then left.

"Bitch, what the fuck took yo' lil' ass so long?" I hissed, feeling sweat slide down my back.

"That nigga was all over me. He got a whole bunch of money trying to flex and shit. The only way I was able to break free of him was because I told him I needed to go to the bathroom to freshen up. He's in his bedroom waiting on me."

"You let this bitch ass nigga be all over you? Are you serious, right now?" I snapped, ready to choke her lil' ass through the window.

She rolled her eyes. "Daddy, get yo' jealous ass up here and let's handle this nigga." She backed away from the window.

I looked both ways making sure nobody was looking. Then I jumped, grabbed the windowsill and hoisted myself up. I used my shoes to climb up. As soon as I got into the window, I wiggled my legs and slid inside. I fell right on the bathroom floor beside the toilet.

Bubbie peeked out of the bathroom door down the hall. She was dressed in just a pair of pink Victoria Secret thongs, and a matching pink halter. I wanted to snap, especially because I could see our baby's bulge in her stomach. In the background, *Moneybagg's Dice Game* beat through the speakers.

"A'ight, Daddy, I'm finna gon' down the hall and into his room. It's the second door on the left. You can go in there and do your thing." She opened the door and slithered out. My eyes were on her ass the entire time. Her cheeks looked hefty like she'd gotten them bitches done or something, but I knew better.

I gave her a three-minute head start, then I was in the hallway with my .40 cocked. I slid with my back against the wall. When I got to the second door, I took a deep breath and placed my hand on the knob. I slowly turned it open, then with blazing speed, I was inside with my gun out, rushing toward the bed. Bubbie was on top of him rubbing his chest with her hands. When she saw me, she punched him as hard as she could in the face and jumped off him.

"His ass knows Mikey real good," she said, standing by the dresser.

Ralphie hurried slid his hand under the pillow. Before I could level my gun to buck at his ass, he was shooting at me. *Blocka! Blocka! Blocka! Blocka!*

Big holes filled the walls, white smoke billowed from the drywall and filled the room with the powdery like substance. He kept shooting his .38 special, *Blocka! Blocka! Click! Click! Click!* He rolled off the bed and started reaching under it. When I saw him coming up with an assault rifle, I let his ass have it.

Bock! Bock! Bock! Bock! Bock! The holes filled the top of his shoulders and cranium. He slumped to the carpet shaking as blood spewed out of him at a rapid pace.

Bubbie came around and stood behind me. "Daddy, Daddy, are you okay?" she asked, shaking like a leaf while looking down at him.

I grabbed her lil' ass by her shirt and pulled her to me. "You always check under the pillow. Anytime you bussing a move on a nigga, you're always supposed to check under the pillows. That's where niggas keep their straps at. Do you hear me?"

She nodded. "Yes, Daddy, yes, I hear you."

"Get dressed and anything you touched wipe it down. We only got about three minutes before the police will be all over this place." While she got dressed and wiped everything down, I took a pillowcase and filled it with the cash that Ralphie had splayed all over the living room table, along with half of brick of China.

When I got back into the room Bubbie was frozen, looking down at Ralphie's body. "Damn, Daddy, it's the first one I've ever seen a death I help cause, fuck him, though." She continued looking down mugging him.

I grabbed her hand and pulled her out of the room. "Let's get the fuck out of here. We gotta go back to the drawing board."

Ghost

Chapter 7

Two weeks later, still neither me or Veronica had heard anything about whether Jahliya was dead or alive. To say I felt lost would have been an understatement. Bubbie had arranged for the hunnit grand payments for both weeks to be paid on time. She said instead of Mikey picking them up himself, he just had her leave the money in a duffle bag inside a locker that was supplied to her at the Greyhound bus station. I didn't know what he was up, or if my sister was even still breathing. The whole situation had me mentally drained. If it was up to me, I felt I coulda easily went on a killing spree in her honor, but Bubbie kept on talking me out of it.

"Daddy, I know you're stressing, right now, but you have to keep the faith. Phoenix, will be here soon. He'll know who exactly to hit and when. Trust me, you just gotta stay the course, and eat somethin'," Bubbie said, as she placed a plate of southern fried chicken, baked macaroni and cheese, collard greens and homemade sweet cornbread in front of me.

Then she poured me a nice glass of Hawaiian Punch with ice cubes in it. The food made my stomach growl and turn again. My mind was too fucked up to be trying to keep it down. She broke off a piece of the chicken and tried to feed me.

"Here, Daddy, just try it," she urged.

It touched my lips, and I turned my head. "Nall, Shawty, I ain't got no appetite for that shit."

"But it's been three days since you've eaten a good meal. You gon' fuck around and pass out. Then what good are you to me, Jahliya, our unborn child, or even Veronica for that matter?"

I shrugged my shoulders. "I don't know, I just ain't feeling that shit, right now, that's all."

"Please, Honey, can you eat some of it for me?" She poked out her little freckled lip.

I couldn't help but soften up a tad. "Come on, Boo."

She smiled and forked up some of the macaroni. She slid the fork into my mouth and fed me. "Tell me if you like it. It's three different kinds of cheeses."

I chewed and tried my best to think about anything else besides vomiting. I kept seeing Jahliya's face. It was making me so sick my stomach. "It's good, baby, you did your thing."

She held the side of my face while I ate. I liked how she mothered me and tried her best to make sure I was always feeling okay. I knew I had to get better at that when it came to her. After all, she was showing that she deserved my love and affection.

"Daddy, do you remember when we were driving to do that lick on Ralphie? I was finna ask you a question, but you told me it would have to wait until later." She broke some of the chicken off the bone and fed it to me.

"Yeah, baby, I remember. What's good?"

"Well, if you cool, I would like to ask my question, right now?"

"Gon' head." I kept chewing the chicken. She really did do her thing. For me, there was nothing like a female who could cook. That cooking shit was definitely a direct route to my heart.

"What I was going to ask was, what happens between us when Tamia steps back into the picture?"

"What do you mean?"

"Well, I know you're really not the type to express your feelings for me and all that. I guess I feel like you honestly do care about me. I just wanted to know when she steps back into the picture, will all that change? I'm letting you know, right now, I will kill her before I let her take you away from me.

You and I are supposed to be together, and we're going to be for a very long time. I understand she is due to have your kid as well, but that don't give her the right to keep up a bunch of bullshit. I love you too much for that shit."

I grabbed a napkin, she took it out of my hand and wiped my mouth for me, then kissed me on the lips, before handing me my juice. I sipped it and set the glass back on the table.

"Bubbie, you and I are good. I ain't got time for that high school drama shit, life is too short. Tamia, just gon' have to accept things the way they are. You the one holding me down. I don't even know where Shawty is."

Bubbie smiled. "And you shouldn't worry about it either, Daddy because I don't need no help caring for you. We got this. That real love always shines a light on the fake. It's always been that way. But just know your Bubbie is, right here and I ain't leaving your side, I refuse to." She kissed my cheek.

The doorbell rang, we both tended to freeze. I had to think about it for a second before it made sense that somebody was actually at the front door. "Come to think of it, why is your mother always gone?"

"Really, somebody ringing the doorbell made you think about asking me that?" She rolled her eyes. She had a habit of doing that. "I don't know she's always traveling, or away on business. I don't be wanting to go away with her, so I stay home. Why is that a big deal to you?"

"Nall, I was just curious. Come on, let's go and see who is at the door." I grabbed my .45 and held it at my side while letting her walk ahead of me. When we got to the door, I side-stepped, and slowly pulled back the curtain, to see what I could see.

On the porch stood Danyelle, she looked frazzled. Her hair was all over the place, and she appeared to have a black eye.

Before I could even think about it twice, I brushed past Bubbie and pulled the door open.

"Lil' cuz, what the fuck happened to you?" I asked, ready to snap.

"Your Auntie happened. She's a freaking psychopath. I swear to God, I'm so sick of her putting her hands on me. I'm not a little girl anymore." She took a seat on Bubbie's sofa and covered her face with both hands.

Bubbie looked up to me. "What you finna do?"

I closed the door and locked it. Then went and sat beside Danyelle on the couch, placing my arm around her neck. "Cuz, why she do this to you?"

Danyelle shook her head and sighed out loud. Before she answered, she looked over to Bubbie. "Say, girl, I know this is your mansion and everything, but would you mind giving me a few minutes to talk with my cousin?"

Bubbie frowned. "Hell, yeah, I mind. That's my man, ain't shit you need to say to him that I can't hear. Me and him don't keep secrets from each other."

Danyelle stared at her in disbelief. "Damn, bitch, it's like that?"

"It's just like that. I don't trust yo' pretty ass, or no other bitch around him for that matter." Bubbie came and stood next to me.

I stood up and took hold of Danyelle's hand. "Look, Bubbie, I'm finna take her downstairs to the den, so I can see what's going on with her and Veronica. I'll be back up in a little while." Before she could answer me, and Danyelle were already on our way past her. I looked over my shoulder at her one time to see her standing at the end of the hall with a look of hatred on her face. The look was almost frightening.

***

"Damn, what's wrong with that bitch, cuz? You fuckin' her that good?" Danyelle asked, sitting on me the couch crossing her thighs, causing her short sundress to raise.

"That ain't yo' bidness, tell me why Veronica whooped yo ass."

She shrugged her shoulders. "I don't know, when we left here, she was saying she was gon' get in my ass for disappearing, but she never got around to it. Then this morning she was making it seem like she wanted me to go to Jackson with her to visit her sister, Roxanne. I told her I wanted to stay in Memphis and do my own thing. She called me ungrateful and said I was just like my father. I said, she was nuts and she went crazy. I woulda had more injuries than this had I not blocked most of her blows. Long story short, she kicked me out and trashed me to my father. He called me all kinds of sluts and said he was coming to pick me up immediately so he could get in my ass as well. I bounced on their asses and here I am. I need to stay with you and Bubbie for a few weeks until I can get myself together. I hope that's cool? It's either here, or the streets."

I didn't have to think about it that long. There was no way, I was finna let Danyelle live on the streets. Besides, I felt it could be cool having two females in the house. I could think of a bunch of ways to keep myself busy, and my mind off Jahliya, and Tamia, if only for a little while. "You good, cuz, you can stay here."

"But you didn't even ask, Bubbie, yet. Ain't she gon' be mad?"

"I don't know, but I don't care either. You ain't finna be ripping and running in no fuckin' streets. It's my job to protect you."

She squealed, jumped up, ran to me and wrapped her arms around my neck. "I love you so much, JaMichael? I knew you was crazy about me." She snuck her face around and kissed my lips. She took my hands off her lower back and placed them on her ass. "I missed you so much, JaMichael. Damn, you, don't have any idea how much." Her tongue wrestled with mine, then she moaned into my mouth.

I tongued her for a moment, then broke out of her embrace. "How did you get over here?"

"I caught an Uber, I paid her, and she's already gone."

"Where are your clothes?"

"I don't have any, I just came with the clothes on my back. Are you mad at me?"

"Nall, you good. Let me go up here so I can holla at her. You should probably catch a small nap, and by the time you wake up, everything should be ironed out. A'ight?"

She nodded and kissed my lips again, sucking longer on the bottom one. She had me rock hard and ready to fuck.

"A'ight cuz, gon' get that bitch mind right. I can tell she don't like me and she's going to be a problem."

"Just do like I said and watch yo' mouth. She's pregnant with my seed. Keep that *bitch* word to yourself."

She looked dumbfounded as I closed the door, and stepped into the hallway, just as Bubbie was taking her ear away from the door.

"I know you didn't just tell that girl, she could stay at my house without asking me?"

I pushed her down the hall a tad. "Fuck is you doing eavesdropping? Do you gotta problem or somethin'?" I asked angry.

"You, damn right I do? How the fuck you gon' just offer my house to somebody else?"

"Shut yo' ass up and let's go talk in the other room." I tried to grab ahold of her wrist.

She smacked my hand away. "Answer my question."

"Fuck was it?"

She flared her nostrils and laughed for a split second. I could tell she was close to losing it. "JaMichael, what gives you the right to tell this bitch she can stay wit' us? Who do you think you are?"

"Bitch, I'm Ghost, that's who I am."

She jerked her head back and rested her hand on her chest. "Oh, so you can check her about calling me a bitch, but it's okay for you to come right behind her and do the same exact thing?"

Damn, I felt stupid, I had to get that bitch word out of my vocabulary, especially when it referred to her or Tamia. They were set to be the mothers of my children. I had to have more respect for them for that fact alone. "Look, I ain't mean to call you no—"

She cut me off. "No real man gon' call his baby mother no bitch, especially when she's pregnant. They would have more respect for her and their child. You need to check yourself, or we finna fight." She threatened.

I mugged her lil' ass, sometimes it annoyed me when she acted tougher than I knew she was. I honored her heart, but sometimes that shit was just annoying. "Bubbie, bring yo' ass here."

She crossed her arms and stood at a safe distance. "Nope."

"Baby, don't play wit' me bring yo' ass here."

She stayed that way for another minute, then sighed, came across the room, and stood in front of me. I could smell her freshly applied Prada perfume, and the hair grease she used. As soon as she was within arm's reach, I grabbed her and held

her by the waist. She looked up at me with her adorable almond eyes.

"Ain't you the one who said we're in this together, and
what's yours is mine, and vice versa?" I asked, bringing her
closer to me.

She shrugged her shoulders. "I don't know, I mighta said
that. What's your point?"

"My point is that my lil' cousin needs shelter, and I'm gon'
give it to her using our shit until she's able to work things out
with my Auntie. As soon as that happens, she'll be on her
way."

"But I don't feel like sharing you, JaMichael. I just got you
all to myself. Now I gotta split your attention between me,
Angel and Danyelle. Man, fuck that, she already makes me so
nervous because of how pretty she is. Plus, I know y'all family's history, and I see the way she looks at you. That girl
wants you, JaMichael. She wants you bad. I don't know if I
can compete with that other shit. You feel what I'm saying?"

I laughed her off and kissed her forehead. "It's me and
you, Boo. Ain't nobody finna break that up I don't care who
they are. You need to get that through your head."

"Maybe I could believe that if you showed me that was the
case in the least bit. So far you ain't did nothing but make me
feel more insecure than I have ever felt in any relationship
prior to you. I mean I don't get it. I am literally trying to do
everything I can to show you, I am all about you, but none of
it seems to be sticking. What is it about me that makes you
wanna shit on me like you do?"

I was taken aback. "You feel like I be shitting on you, for
real?"

"Yep, anytime I express my love for you, you, don't ever
reciprocate or make me feel like you feel half the same way
as I do. Do you have any idea how much that hurts my

feelings?" She dropped a tear, and quickly wiped it away, turning her back to me.

I slid behind her and pulled her back to my chest. "Baby, I'm sorry. Do you hear me?"

She kept her silence for a moment. "You're sorry for what, JaMichael?"

"I'm sorry for making you feel like I be shitting on you. I swear I don't mean to be on that. I just been going through a lot, and I guess somewhere down the line, I haven't taken the time to really pay attention to how I've been acting toward you, I'm sorry for that."

She tensed up, grabbed my hands and made me wrap them around her even tighter. She was like a little girl trying her best to be a woman. I don't know why I found that so sexy, but I did. "JaMichael, do you really care about me, or am I just your baby mother to be?"

"Come on, boo, why would you ask me some shit like that?"

"Answer the question?"

"Yeah, I care about you. You're in my heart, and it's in me to hold you down. We're riding for each other, right?"

"Right, that's what we're supposed to be doing anyway."

"Well, then that's what it is. I love you girl, and I ain't going nowhere. We in this shit together."

She turned around and hugged my neck. "I love you, too, so so much. Okay, Daddy, now we can go tell Danyelle, she can stay here for a few weeks. I'm good to go now." She kissed my lips and hugged me as tight as she could.

Ghost

Chapter 8

I don't know why every time I tried to do the right thing, the devil always had a plan to try and ruin what I was trying to accomplish. Two weeks had gone by with Danyelle staying with us, and all had been well. The girls were getting along, and the house was peaceful. We still had yet to hear anything about my sister's situation, but Phoenix was set to roll back into town any day now, so I remained optimistic.

It was a stormy Friday night, it had been raining the entire day, and Bubbie was tired of being in the house, so she proposed that we take Angel out to see a movie, which we did. Halfway through the movie Bubbie started feeling sick and told me that she felt like she had the worst migraine she'd ever had her entire life. She needed to get home asap, so she could go to sleep.

When we got to the house, Angel was already knocked out in my arms and Bubbie seemed to be leaning on me for support keeping herself up. I carried Angel to her bedroom and tucked her in. Candy had said, she'd be picking her up the following Monday because she'd been out of town for one reason or the other. Bubbie snapped when she found this out because Candy never even told us she was leaving or expressed any concern about not seeing her daughter for nearly a month. I found that odd but kept calm. Bubbie snapped and caused herself to have a headache.

When I made it upstairs to the room we slept in, she was sliding her nightgown over her naked frame. She crawled across the bed and waited for me to place her feet in my lap. I kissed each toe, then rubbed both feet for an entire hour, until she fell asleep. Then I pulled the comforter over her and kissed her forehead. I figured I'd take a quick shower and get into bed, but when I made it into the hallway, there was Danyelle standing a short distance away in a pair of red lace boy shorts that were all in her sex lips. Her thick thighs were hefty and exposed. She wore a white tank top, her nipples were fully engorged and pressing through the fabric. She motioned with her finger for me to come to her.

I closed the door to the room and stepped up to her. "What's up?" I could feel that forbidden blood inside of me bubbling.

She looked over my shoulder and stepped on her tippy toes. Her lips brushed against my ear canal. "Where yo' baby mama?"

"Why?"

She sucked her bottom lip and looked over my shoulder again. Then took her left hand and cuffed my piece. "Cause, JaMichael, I been as good as I could. I need some of this, Cuz. I need you to treat me real fast. My pussy's boiling for you, please don't say no." She took my hand and slid them into her tight panties. I could feel her lips on the tip of my fingers. They felt hot and rubbery. Then she was running her tongue around inside my ear, making me harder than a block of wood. "Come on, JaMichael, take me to the den, Cuz." She jumped up on me and wrapped her thighs around my waist.

The next thing I knew, I was carrying her inside the den and tossing her on the Futon. I kicked the door closed and fell between her thick thighs.

She moaned as soon as she felt my weight between her legs. "Damn, JaMichael, I need you so bad. I swear I been doing everythang I can to be a good girl but seeing you with Bubbie be driving me crazy." She pulled me down and kissed my lips. She sucked the top one first, then the bottom one. Her tongue searched for mine, when she found it, she started moaning and humping into me.

I could feel her heat all over my stomach. I slid down her body and opened her thighs roughly. Her pussy was stuffed into the small panties. Each lip was visible on the sides of the crotch band. I sniffed her, then sucked on each one, before licking up and down the band of her panties.

She arched her back. "Unnhhh, JaMichael, here you go turning me out again. Damn, I love you so much."

I yanked her material to the side roughly, spread open her fold and trapped her clit with my lips, suckling like I was trying to draw some milk from her. She bucked like crazy and stuffed my face further between her thighs. Her scent was heavy. The further my nose went into her gap, the crazier it drove me. I licked up and down her slit, at the same time running two digits in and out of her tight box.

"I'm finna make you cum, right now, lil' Cuz. I can feel this pussy quivering. You wanna cum, don't you? Tell me." I was sucking her clit again.

"I wanna cum, I wanna cum! Oh, fuck, I love you so much! Uuunnhhh shit!" She opened her thick thighs as far as she could and humped all over my tongue and nose.

I kept on licking and slurping, I wanted to get it all. Her juices were driving me crazy. She continued to buck and whimper. I flipped her on her stomach and sucked each thick ass cheek. Then spread them, sending my tongue into circles all around her rosebud. Then I was back to sucking that cat and fingering her at full speed. My piece was hard as hell. I couldn't wait to get inside that box. She came grabbing a handful of the sheets. Then she turned so she could sit on her ass. She grabbed my piece and brought it to her mouth, deep throating me to the best of her abilities.

Now it was my turn to moan and allow my eyes to roll into the back of my head. I clutched the sides of the Futon, and slow stroked her lips. It started feeling so good I was afraid, I was going to buss too early. So, I pulled out, picked her lil' ass up and tossed her on the bed. Then flipped her over and rubbed my dick up and down her groove. She was so wet her juices were running down her thighs, all the way to her knees on each side. I stopped and took a second to eat that pussy from the back.

It didn't last long before she was cumming again. "Now, JaMichael, please fuck me now!" She reached for me. When she took a hold of it, she stuffed herself and leaned forward on her elbows. "Beat this pussy, Cuz, please beat it up."

I slammed forward hard, took a hold of her hips, and long stroked her with no remorse. I kept pulling her back to me every time I slammed forward. I needed to make sure, she was taking all the dick. Since she wanted to play in my lane, I was gon' make sure she got the full effect.

She closed her eyes and beat her tiny fists on the Futon bed, slamming back, taking as much pipe as she could. She grabbed the pillow and screamed into it, cumming, and shaking as if she were having a seizure. The feeling of her climax brought mine to the forefront. I grabbed a hold of all that meat on her ass and pulled her to me, while I came back to back. My jets attacked her walls over and over. She scooted all the way forward until I fell on top of her, then she turned around, grabbed my piece, and started sucking her juices off it hungrily.

I laid back with my hands behind my head groaning. "Get it, Danyelle, that's my baby."

Those words seemed to egg her on. She started sucking faster and faster. When she got me good and hard, she climbed on top of me and slid me back into her box. She took hold of my shoulders and rode me with her head tilted backward.

"This my dick! This my dick, uh, JaMichael! You took my virginity! This my dick!" She sucked on my neck and rode me for thirty full minutes, causing me to cum inside of her twice more, before she collapsed on top of me, breathing hard.

***

I showered before sneaking back into Bubbie's room. I felt low like I'd betrayed her. I hated myself for not having dick control. Veronica always told me that my father Taurus was a ladies man. I wondered what that meant in its entirety, and if he'd ever had problems controlling his man down low. I really needed to speak with and maybe even see my father. I had so many questions for him. I climbed into the bed before I could get into it good enough.

Bubbie woke up and pulled the covers off her head. "Ja-Michael, is that you?"

"Yeah, boo, go back to sleep."

"You just now getting into the bed? What time is it?"

"It's late, now go back to sleep."

She sat up, grabbed her phone and cut it on so she could see the clock, then set it back down on its face. "Boy, it's three o'clock. Where the fuck you been at?"

I thought of a hundred lies I coulda told her right then, but none of them rolled off my tongue quick enough. "Baby, I just wanna hold you. Come here."

She threw the covers off her and got out of the bed. She stood at the end of it. "JaMichael, get yo' ass up and drop yo' boxers."

"What?"

"Boy, stop playin' wit' me. You heard what I said. Now bring yo' ass over here and do like I said," she said forcefully.

I stood staring at her for a moment. Then I just came on over. I knew I didn't still smell like Danyelle's pussy because I'd showered real good, so I wasn't worried about nothin'. I pulled down my boxers right in front of her. "Here man, now what?"

She came closer and dropped to one knee. She took hold of my piece and sniffed him. Then looked up at me and frowned. "You got in the shower, for what?"

"I was sticky, I needed a shower. Why you making such a big deal out of nothing?"

She stroked my piece and kept looking at it, not at me. Even though me and Danyelle had done our thing for every bit of three hours, and my shit was sore. Her soft stroking caused him to rise to his fullest potential.

"Did you leave this house?"

"Nall, why you acting so weird?"

She kissed the head and sucked only it into her mouth for about thirty seconds, then she popped it out with a loud noise. "You fucked somebody tonight, JaMichael? Be honest."

I smacked her hand away. "I just told yo' silly ass I ain't even left the house tonight. So, who could I have fucked?" I asked, hoping she would just let the matter go. I was tired and I needed to get some sleep, fast.

She smacked her lips. "You know what, I'ma give you the benefit of the doubt this time. Get yo' ass in the bed so you can hold me. Oh, and JaMichael, if I ever find out you're lying about tonight, nigga I got something for yo' ass. Trust me when I tell you this." She clicked off the lamp and crawled across the bed until she was lying next to me. Then she turned on her side and slammed her ass into my lap. "Now hold me and goodnight.

I couldn't do nothin' but feel like a bitch ass nigga for cheating on her. Damn, I could tell Bubbie was made for me, but I still missed Tamia. I also knew that I would have to have some more of Danyelle real soon. She had a lil' box on her that I was becoming addicted to.

I never understood why men could have a down ass woman at home, one that was a freak, his entire match, and all of that, but still couldn't turn down the next bitch's pussy. I mean Bubbie was bad and fine from head to toe. She was loyal for as far as I could tell. Had plenty of money and was 'bout that life. Yet, even though I sincerely cared about her whole-heartedly, I knew I still craved other pussy. I felt fucked up, I needed to see my father so we could have a long talk. I needed to understand myself as a man.

I kissed the side of Bubbie's forehead. "I love you, Bubbie, I mean that shit."

"Yeah, that's cool, JaMichael. I'll talk to you in the morning, Jehovah's willing. Goodnight!"

Ghost

Chapter 9

I jumped off the picnic table as soon as Phoenix pulled his drop-top, red Benz, into the parking lot of the Lakefront. Before he could cut the ignition, I was on him. "Phoenix, where the fuck is my sister? I know you know where that nigga Mikey is holding her."

He stepped out of his whip and pulled his Ray-Bans off his caramel face. The sunlight reflected off the top of his deep waves. "Before we do anythang nigga, I'ma need you to back yo' ass up a few notches. Don't be running up on me like you, 'bout that there. Nigga shit ain't sweet." He stepped back just a tad.

I was able to see the handle of his gun poking through his shirt. He was so brazen to have a Tech-9 laid directly on the passenger seat. I guess he thought I was supposed to be spooked or something, but all I felt was anger and frustration.

"Nigga, fuck you. You think you the only one strapped?" I asked mugging him with intense hatred. I didn't like him, or nobody that was part of the Duffle Bag Cartel. I felt all those dudes were shiesty and always up to no good. I had two .40s on my hip and a .380 in my ankle. I was ready to take it wherever he wanted to take it.

Bubbie rushed over and stood in between us. She pushed her arms out the long way. "Y'all need to chill. Ain't neither one of us the enemy to the other, so fall the fuck back, both of you."

Phoenix continued to mug me, and I never took my eyes of hatred off him either. In fact, I moved Bubbie out of the way and stepped in his face. "Where the fuck is, Jahliya?"

He clenched his jaw and looked deep into my eyes for a long time before responding, "Say, Mane, on the strength that I know you're going through a lot, I'm going to let you have whatever this is. But only because I got word directly from your father to do what I need to do with you."

I was frozen. How the fuck had he gotten word from my father? The only way he would have been able to do that is if he'd spoken to him directly, or if he'd gone to see him. "Fuck you mean you got word directly from my father?"

"JaMichael, you need to understand I'm not your enemy. I am more connected to you than you think. But we can get into all of that shit later."

"Nall, nigga, we finna get into this, right now. What the fuck are you talking about?"

Bubbie stepped back in between us. "Baby, don't freak out okay, what I'm about to tell you is going to sound crazy as fuck. Please just know I only found this out literally today. So, I've been in the dark as well."

"Fuck is y'all talking about?" I looked back and forth from Bubbie to Phoenix. I was getting more and more angry by the second.

"Listen, JaMichael, word is that Mikey is supposed to have killed Jahliya and dumped her body in a creek. Now I don't know how true that is, but I got a couple of killas that work directly under Mikey that are more loyal to me than they are to him. They gave me three locations where he might be holding her if she's still alive. I can't explain to you just yet how Taurus comes into all of this, but when the time is right you will know. In the meantime, Bruh, I'm riding wit' you one hunnit percent until we find her. But I'ma need you to trust me because we finna have to fuck some dudes over along the way. You cool with that?"

"Nigga this is my heart we're talking about. You know damn well I'm down for whatever, as long as I get her back. Nothing else matters."

"That's all I'm talking about. I got some shit being set in motion. I need a few days before I can clarify everything. I'ma be in touch as soon as I'm ready to roll out. I'm letting you know, right now, shit is about to get real bloody lil' homie."

I felt like I was about to have an anxiety attack. I kept imagining Jahliya floating lifeless in a creek somewhere. The image was killing my soul. I don't even know where they came from, but all of a sudden tears were running down my cheeks, and my throat felt like it had huge lumps in it.

"Dawg, how soon will it be before you can find out if she's alive or not?"

"You just gotta give me a few hours to find that out. Word is that Mikey lamping down in Texas, Cloverland. That's is Houston. My cousin Shemar down there. If there is anything new, we need to know about this situation, by Mikey being in his city he gon' have the full information. He don't be with that fuck shit either. He don't like them Duffle Bag niggas because of a stunt they tried to pull when I was out of town a few weeks ago. Just try yo' best to rest easy. We on bidness in a minute, trust that lil' homie."

He extended his hand and it took a while for me to shake it. But I did, and when I did, I held it tight. "Listen here, Phoenix, I don't know why you're having a change of heart. But I'm telling you, right now, if Mikey or any of your crew hurt my sister, nigga after I make all of them pay, I'm coming for you, and everybody you love. That threatening shit ain't in my blood, nor my heart neither. I mean everything I'm saying." I released my grip and turned my back on him. "Get up with me as soon as you know something. Let's go, Bubbie."

"Nigga, you just don't get it do you?" Phoenix asked.

I stopped mid-stride and turned around. I was hoping he was getting ready to take shit where I needed it to go. I was heated and needed to let off some steam. I wanted to whoop his ass, then pop him more than a few times. "Excuse me?"

He walked halfway to me and stopped. "I don't give a fuck, about Mikey or them Duffle Bag niggas. That punk just tried to do the same shit wit' my daughter that he's doing to your sister. All because of a female, so trust me when I tell you, we got the same goal. I wanna get your sister back, then I wanna annihilate that nigga in the most gruesome way possible."

I listened to him with an open heart and mind. I still couldn't decide if I trusted him or not, but what could I do? He had more inside information than I did. All I cared about was finding my sister. If Phoenix was the key, then I would have to play my role accordingly.

"Well, like I said, get at me as soon as you know what route we should take. I'm ready for war, know that."

He nodded, jumped into his Benz, and sped away.

Bubbie walked up to me with her face in a ball of fury. "What the fuck was that about, Daddy?" she asked pointing to Phoenix's Benz, as it drove away.

"What are you talking about now, Bubbie?" I didn't feel like arguing with her lil' ass. I kept thinking about Jahliya, and what Phoenix had said he'd heard Mikey had done to her.

"I'm talking about the fact that my cousin is honestly trying his best to have your back, and all you're doing is making threats about what you're going to do to him if things don't go right. News flash, not everything can go right, and the world is bigger than your situation. I know that sucks to hear, but it's the truth." She placed a strand of her curly hair behind her ears.

The lakefront was starting to fill up with people. There were a bunch of them grabbing their beach towels and picnic baskets. As they got out of their cars, they took time to glance over at me and Bubbie arguing. I really didn't feel like making a spectacle. My new phone buzzed. A text from Tamia came across the screen. My face formed an instant smile.

"Look, Bubbie, I still find it hard to believe that Phoenix ain't know nothing about Mikey getting ready to kidnap my sister. Every muthafucka in Memphis knows he and Mikey are thick as thieves. They do everythang together. Now he supposed to be working with me to get her back. "Yeah, a'ight, I guess we finna see ain't we?"

"Who the fuck just text you?" she asked, taking a step forward, shielding her eyes from the sun.

I returned the text to Tamia letting her know I would be meeting her at Yvonne's Butt Outs, in about ten minutes. "Don't worry about it, just a business contact."

Bubbie jerked her head back and placed her hand on her waist. "Negro, I know damn well that you ain't just tell me not to worry about whose hitting up your phone. You got me all the way fucked up. Now tell me who it is."

"Anyway, I'm finna roll over here and handle this bidness, drop me off at my truck," I ordered and opened the passenger door to her black on black Lexus.

She stood out of the car talking to herself for a second. Then she smiled and made her way around the whip. She opened the driver's door and took her seat. I expected her to start the ignition, instead, she reached across the console, and slapped the shit out of me. *Whack!*

That shit hurt my face so bad my eyes watered. I reacted by grabbing her lil ass by the throat. Then I remembered she was pregnant and a female, so I let her go. "Bitch don't be smacking me, that's your last fuckin' warning! Now take me to my truck."

"Fuck you, Ghost! Who the fuck were you texting?" Her face was getting redder.

"Shawty, start this car, we'll talk about this shit later when I get back."

"JaMichael, Taurus Stevens, if you don't tell me who the fuck just hit you up, so help me God, I'm finna buss you in yo' shit. You gon' have to whoop my ass in front of all of these people at this beach. Now, who the fuck was it?"

I sat there irritated as fuck. I wasn't with all this baby mama drama shit. I was too young for it and on top of that our baby hadn't even got here yet. "Bubbie, start the engine before you make me miss my appointment."

She reached across and tried her best to yank the phone out of my hand. I moved just in time and popped her on the back of her shit. This made her go crazy. She turned sideways in her seat and swung three blows. Two of them caught me in the jaw, and the last one I blocked before I slapped the shit out of her. Her head hit the horn and made about ten people look toward our car.

She held her face. "You, bitch ass nigga. I can't believe you just hit me knowing I'm pregnant?" Now she was swinging wildly and fucking me up. She even laid with her head against the driver's door and kicked me a bunch of times.

I grabbed her ankles and punched her as hard as I could in each of her thick thighs. I knew that shit had to hurt because she groaned in pain. "Start the muthafuckin' car and let's get the fuck out of here. Now!" I snapped.

"Fuck you!" She grabbed the keys out of the ignition, opened the door, and ran toward the lake with them.

When she got all the way across the sand, she cocked back and threw her keys as far into the water as she could. I watched them splash in grayish blue liquid. By the time she turned around I was already out of the parking lot. Her house was only five blocks away. That was a short distance for me. She located me and tried her best to run after me while holding her belly.

I was already texting Tamia's letting her know to meet me at Yvonne's in fifteen minutes instead of ten. When Bubbie caught up to me she was out of breath and had tears in her eyes. "Why are you doing this to me, Daddy? I thought I was your baby?"

"You are my baby, Bubbie, but you are tripping. I ain't doing shit to you, I gotta handle this bidness."

She rested her hands on her knees. "Are you serious it's only a business contact?"

I nodded. "Yeah, that's all it is."

She struggled to breathe. "You sho' it ain't no bitch?"

"Nall, it ain't no bitch," I lied.

"And you would never lie to me?"

I kept walking. "Nall, Shawty, I wouldn't."

"You're fuckin' lying right now, JaMichael! I know you're going to meet up with that bitch, Tamia!"

I ignored her ass and kept walking. Mrs. Jamie, my old twelfth-grade writing teacher just so happened to be rolling by. She brought her car to a halt and rolled the window down to her Jetta. "Hey, Mr. Stevens, long time no see," she said, smiling and looking sexy. I had a thing for her back in high school, especially when I found out my teacher was a freak.

"What's good, Mrs. Jamie?"

"On my way to the beach to get some sun. What are you up to?" She glanced over to Bubbie.

Bubbie took off her wedge and ran into the street. She raised it over her head and brought it down as hard as she could on to Mrs. Jamie's white hood to her car. "Bitch, can't you see he's in the middle of something? Get the fuck out of here!" she screamed and brought the wedge down again.

Mrs. Jamie's eyes got bucked. She backed up her car and pulled around Bubbie. But not before giving me the call me sign? Then she was off.

Bubbie stood in the middle of the street with her chest heaving up and down. "Why JaMichael, why do you need to go see, Tamia? Are you finna fall back in love with her?" she cried, limping because she only had one shoe on.

I walked off. "Bubbie, you need to grow the fuck up. That's my baby mother, too. I gotta see what's good with her. That's my job and you know it is."

She ran and caught up. "I'm going wit' you then. That bitch needs to know you and I are together now. I don't want her thinking it's sweet. She should know how we feel about each other, don't you think?"

I kept walking because I didn't know what to say about that. I loved Bubbie, I truly did, but I also loved, and cared about Tamia. She was my first love. There was no way I could just kick her to the curb like that. I still didn't know if I would ever be able to admit to her that I had strong feelings for Bubbie. I felt like I was crossing her to even be thinking some shit like that. She and I had been through so much together ever since we were kids, but lately, so had Bubbie and me.

Bubbie stopped mid-pace and slumped her shoulders. "Oh, my God. You don't give a fuck about me, JaMichael, its always been Tamia." She closed her eyes, turned around, and began walking back in the direction of her Lexus.

I knew I shoulda stopped her, but I wasn't mature enough to. Besides I was curious to see how Tamia was doing. I stopped to look over my shoulder back to her one time, her shoulders slumped as she walked slowly to her car. I continued walking in the other direction.

Chapter 10

Tamia jumped in my arms and held me as tight as she could with tears rolling down her face. " Damn, I missed you, Ja-Michael. I swear to God I missed you so much. I never thought I would see you again. All that bitch, Yin, and Grizzly kept talking about was they were going to kill you and Getty as soon as they got those diamonds. I was praying they never got them back, but then again, I knew you would outsmart them. Fuck, I missed you." She hugged me again this time she stayed attached for what seemed like five full minutes. I held her in my arms, I didn't care if the entire restaurant was watching us.

When we broke our embrace, I pulled out her chair and allowed her to sit down, before I scooted it forward for her. "Tamia, where were you?"

She frowned. "*Tamia!* Since when you start calling me by my first name? What happened to, baby or boo?"

"Baby, where were you this whole time?"

She smiled. "Now that's more like it." She reached across the table and took hold of my hand. "With Chino at one of his duck offs in North Memphis. Me and my mother really ain't seeing eye to eye ever since y'all got down. So, I just been chilling wit' my cousin. He been taking good care of me and making sure that I'm straight at all times. That boy got like three maids at his Penthouse that work in shifts." She rubbed the top of my left hand. "Where have you been?"

I sat back in my chair and flared my nostrils. "It don't even matter. I hope you know that I ain't cool with this nigga putting you up and shit. I don't give a fuck if he's your cousin or not. I don't need no help taking care of my woman."

"Baby, it's not like that. He just knew I was in a messed up position. So, he stepped in and did what he was supposed to do. After all, I am his little cousin."

"I don't give no fuck? You're my responsibility. I'll take care of you. Matter of fact, now that we're here, we need to discuss what we finna do. You ain't going back over there. Ain't no need for you, too."

Tamia lowered her head and sighed. "JaMichael, it's not that simple."

"What the fuck are you talking about? All you gotta do is go back there and pack your shit. We finna go and get a Telly or something."

"Wait a minute, you sidestepped the shit out of my question. Where have you been for the past few weeks?"

"That shit don't even matter."

"It doesn't matter, why doesn't it? You've been quizzing me ever since we stepped foot in this restaurant. I've had to answer your questions. What makes you think you aren't going to have to answer mine?"

I sat back and rubbed my hand over my waves. "Man, I been trying my best to lay low. I already knew Veronica's crib was going to be hot as a muthafucka. Not only with them Duffle Bag niggas, but also with the police. So, I—"

"Oh my, God! What the fuck is this bitch doing here?" Tamia said, she stood up and balled both of her fists.

Bubbie stepped into the restaurant and looked around until she spotted us. As soon as she did, she smiled and began walking over to the table. When she got there, she leaned down and kissed me on the cheek. "Hey, Daddy, I'm sorry I'm late."

Tamia mugged her, then me. "What the fuck is going on here?"

Bubbie laughed. "Ah, okay, I see I musta got here kinda early. My nigga ain't had the chance to tell you that he and I are together now?"

Tamia looked down at me. "What is she talking about, JaMichael?"

I scooted my chair back, stood up, grabbed Bubbie by the forearm, and dragged her lil' ass across the room toward the bathroom. I didn't even give a fuck, I pushed her inside the men's room and jacked her up against the wall. "What the fuck are you doing here?"

"I'm here because I'm supposed to be here. My Daddy is here, I thought we were in this together? If that's the case, that means there's supposed to be no separating us. Not even when you wanna be alone with, Tamia. Fuck that!" She flared her nostrils and lowered her eyes.

"Bubbie, listen to me, baby. You seem like you're turning psycho. I'ma need you to chill yo' lil' ass out. You're smothering me." I let her go and got ready to leave out of the bathroom.

She grabbed my arm and yanked me back. "*Psycho*, nigga you ain't even began to understand what psycho mean. You belong to me. If you didn't want me to be psycho, you shoulda never got me pregnant. But now that you did, I'm finna be psycho over your ass every second of every day until you start feeling the same way about me. I'm not finna let no female steal you away from me like my father allowed his side bitch to take him away from our family. I'm finna stay on yo' ass, JaMichael. I'll kill Tamia before I let her have you. If you think I'm playing you're about to be in for a rude awakening."

I snatched my arm away from her. "Bubbie, listen to me," I said as calm as I possibly could. "I don't know what the fuck your mother went through. Nor do I know what your father put you through. That shit ain't got nothing to do with me. Don't nobody own me. I got two baby mamas, it's my responsibility to make sure both of y'all are straight. If she was in here talking this same shit, I would be on her ass, too. You gotta get over our relationship because it's going to stay in existence. You get that?"

She looked into my eyes and smiled. "Yeah, JaMichael, I get that." She wiped her tears away. "Gon' head and holla at her. It's good, I'll be waiting at home when you get back. I love you, Daddy." She kissed my cheek and walked out of the bathroom ahead of me.

I stood there for a second trying to gather myself. When another dude stepped into the bathroom I snapped out of my zone, and back into the restaurant. Lucky for me, Tamia, was still waiting at the table. She was eating chicken salad, with ranch dressing.

"You get all of that figured out?"

I pulled out my chair and sat in it. "Yeah, we just needed to iron out a few wrinkles, nothing major."

"So, that's where you been this whole time? You been laid up at her mansion playing, Daddy?" She scoffed and drank from her glass of Apple juice.

"I don't need you getting on that bullshit, too, Tamia. You know it ain't even like that." I felt myself getting a headache.

"I ain't tripping, I mean after all she is having your back as well, right?"

"Right."

She snickered. "Yeah, well, I hope you know I don't have no plans being part of this circus you're creating. I deserve better than to be with a man who gotta spread his focus out on any other female outside of me. I am a queen, if you can't treat me exactly like that, I don't want to deal with you at all. You can have her. I mean that, too." She got lost in a short day-dream, then went right back to eating her salad.

I looked around the dimly lit restaurant that specialized in down-home soul food. It smelled amazing. Every table I looked at were chowing down on Yvonne's home-cooked meals. It was southern cooking at its best.

"Tamia, let me ask you a question?"

She wiped her mouth on a napkin. "Gon' head."

"Do you love me? I mean really love me to the point where you would do anything for me?"

She shrugged her shoulders. "I really love you, I have loved you ever since we were little kids. I don't love you enough that I would jeopardize my own dignity or womanhood. I love myself more than I love anybody else. I don't mean that in a selfish sense. I mean, I refuse to compromise my values or my worth as a woman. I will not be part of this charade. Leaving you will be the hardest part for me, but I would do it in a heartbeat. I wouldn't have any other choice. Does that answer your question?"

I sat there with my head down. "If you were in my position, what would you do?"

She shook her head. "I don't think if I were a boy, I would have ever been that reckless. You had so much going for you. I don't understand how you wound up in the position you're in."

"That ain't what the fuck I asked you."

"Let me finish." She exhaled loudly. "JaMichael, you finna have to let somebody go, it's as simple as that. There is no way you are going to be able to keep two women, especially if one of the two you're banking on keeping is me. I refuse to settle. As much as it hurts me to tell you that, it's the truth."

"A'ight, so what are you asking me to do?"

"You have to choose, baby. Are you going to be with me or her? If you choose me, I want you to do it in front of her. That way I know you actually did it. If you choose her, you can walk away from me, right now, we can go our separate ways. Well never have to speak again. I can say for certain, I will never love any man as much as I loved you, but I will have to chop it up and accept that you had to do what you had to do." She swallowed and her eyes became misty. "So, what are you going to do?"

"Fuck, Tamia, I don't know. I guess I need to think about it because either way, I'm shitting on a woman that is about to have my child."

"Oh, no you not. If you don't choose me, I'm letting you know, right now, I will not be having this baby. There is no way that I'm going to wind up a statistic. That can't happen. I will only have the child of my husband. My child will grow up with both of its parents. I refuse to compromise those values or stipulations. So, I'ma ask you again, what are you going to do?"

***

I didn't make it to Bubbie's mansion until about eight o'clock that night. Me and Tamia had sat parked overlooking the lakefront while we had a nice long talk. In the end, I was able to see where she was coming from, and for some reason I respected it. She convinced me that she was right. Just being able to have a casual conversation with her was mature, and intelligence pushed me more in her direction. I still left her presence feeling lost, and confused, but I knew because of the conversation I had with her, I was one step closer to making a better decision.

Bubbie was waiting on the couch for me when I got in. She was sitting across from Angel. Angel was laid on her stomach snoring lightly. Bubbie got up and came over to me. She stepped on her tippy toes and kissed my cheek. "How are you feeling, Daddy?"

I kissed her back and stepped past her. I took a seat on the same sofa as Angel and rubbed her back. "Where is, Danyelle?"

Bubbie pointed downstairs. "You didn't answer my question." She grabbed a plate of food out of the refrigerator and placed it into the microwave.

"I'm good, but we definitely gotta talk."

She smiled. "Nall, not tonight, we can do that in the morning. Phoenix, said he'll be here in about an hour or so. He wants you to be ready to ride out."

My heart skipped a beat. "Did he find, Jahliya? What did he say to you?"

"He ain't tell me nothin' more than that. I was told to relay that message. I did my part, that's that. What do we gotta talk about anyway? That bitch, Tamia done got all in your head or something?" The microwave beeped, she pulled my food out and set it on the table.

There was no way I could even think about eating. Phoenix had told me he wasn't gon' link up with me for a few days. I was praying he hadn't got some bad news back about Jahliya, and he wanted to tell me that shit face to face. If that was the case, I was getting ready to snap the fuck out.

"Ain't nobody got in my head, Bubbie. Me and Tamia just had some grown people talk today. You know the kind of talks that we don't have."

"What you mean by that, JaMichael? You trying to say she's more mature than me or something?"

I shook my head. "Bubbie, I don't know what I'm saying. But you and I do need to sit down and really talk about what our future is going to be like before and after this baby arrives. We ain't did that yet, and we are running out of time."

She seasoned my lasagna and spread butter over the garlic bread. "A'ight, JaMichael, well, we might as well get it out of the way then. What do you want to discuss about the future?" She rolled her eyes and pulled out a chair so she could sit across from me. I was about to go in on her ass, but Phoenix started ringing the doorbell. She jumped up and stared at me for a brief moment. "If you think, you're about to leave me behind for a situation you think is going to be easier we are about to have serious problems." She slammed the chair into the table and walked off to answer the door.

That same night, we jumped into Phoenix's Bentley, and rolled straight to Houston without making any stops? We didn't even say a word to each other the whole way. We just sat back and listened to *Moneybagg*, and *Lil Baby* serenade the speakers. It took us a nice minute to get to our destination. The whole time I couldn't get Jahliya, Tamia, or Bubbie off my mind. I felt like I was going crazy.

Chapter 11

"JaMichael, I know you might be thinking I should know about these Texas niggas down here 'cause they fuck with the Duffel Bag Cartel, but I don't. Mikey didn't link up with these niggas until me and him had a falling out, so I'm just as lost as you," Phoenix whispered into my ear. He poured seven grams of Peruvian Flake onto a mirror, separated it into eight lines, and took two of them one at a time up each nostril. He gagged and sounded like he was about to throw up.

I jumped back and looked him over like he was crazy. "What the fuck is wrong with you?"

His eyes were watery. He held his nostrils together and looked across the table at me. Then he pushed the mirror my way. "Shit, this just that piy yow, right there. Here, it's your turn."

I moved the mirror from in front of me. "Nigga, I don't get down. I ain't got no habits, and I ain't trying to get none either."

He laughed and looked behind him at the two massive bodyguards standing behind our table. "Uh, JaMichael, we need to get in so we can holla at Shemar? Ain't no muthafucka finna get past these two big ass niggas unless they hitting this powder. It's either this kind or that dog food. Which would you prefer?" He pulled a package of China White out of his pocket and flicked it with his fingernail. It was sealed in aluminum foil.

"I definitely ain't fuckin' with that. You gon' have to give me that other shit."

"That's what I thought." He handed me a rolled-up fifty-dollar bill and placed the mirror back in front of me.

I lowered my head and took a line hard through my right nostril. I coughed, gagged and threw up right there on the side of the couch. Seconds later, I was so high I could hear my heart pounding in my chest, but it sounded like it was in my ears. I felt giddy and numb, there was a steady drip down the back of my throat.

"A'ight, come on, lil', bruh. You got one more line, then you're through."

I was already fucked up. I leaned my head and took another line. Tooted it hard and threw up right where I had the first time. I stood up, two females with mops, and spray came and cleaned up my mess while I looked them over, sipping on a bottle of Hennessey.

Phoenix rose as well and patted my shoulder. "That's what's up, Ghost. A'ight, we clear to roll to the back of the club so we can holla at Shemar now, come on."

I followed Phoenix and the two big bodyguards followed us. Now that I was high, I was paranoid as a muthafucka. I didn't know nothing about Houston. I didn't know who this nigga Shemar was beefing with, or if he had a bunch of enemies that were looking to come and holla at his ass tonight while me and Phoenix were here fuckin' wit' him? I just wanted to get the fuck out of his city, and back to Memphis where I knew all the hoods like the back of my hand.

The strip club was dimly lit. It had four mini-stages inside it, and one big main attraction stage where there was a dark-skinned sistah going to work alongside a thick ass Asian bitch. They were grinding all over each other and pouring champagne on each other's asses. Two of the mini-stages were vacant, and the two that were occupied had a redbone on one, and a caramel sistah on the other. Both were doing their thang. It smelled like perfume, weed smoke, and alcohol. It seems as if it was packed.

We were led down a narrow hallway that traveled past the bathrooms. We came to an exit sign and stepped past it on to a stairwell that had two more huge bodyguards that looked like they shoulda been working for the WWE as wrestlers. We took the steps up two flights and came to another door that was guarded by just one, armed bodyguard. He looked us up and down, before stepping to the side. The guards led us through the door, and into a hallway that stopped at Shemar's office. In front of his office was a thick ass dark-skinned female with a pretty face, and a tight ass dress on. What I found particularly odd about her was the fact that she had a gun in each hand.

Phoenix stepped forward and kissed her on each cheek. "Nicki, how you doing, Sis?"

She shook her head. "Don't nothing move but the money." She nodded at me. "This Taurus son?"

Phoenix nodded. "Yep, can't you tell?"

She came and looked me over closely. "Yeah, I can tell by his face. These cheekbones—smile boy."

I frowned first, then gave her ass a lil' smile even though I didn't feel like doing it.

She nodded. "Yeah, he got them deep ass dimples just like his damn daddy. I bet he got plenty of hoes, don't you?"

I shook my head. "Nall."

She turned up her face sideways. "Yeah, right, well give me a hug anyway. You can call me, Nicki. Me and yo' old man go way back. I used to fuck wit' him on that level."

I slipped my arms past her lil' waist and hugged her. She felt strapped and oh so soft. She even smelled good. "Damn."

She laughed and backed away from me. "Y'all come on, Shemar waiting for you two."

She turned around and knocked on the door twice. She kept looking me in my face. "Was your mother Princess, or Blaze?"

"Blaze," I returned.

"Yeah, I figured, you look just like her, too." She stroked the side of my face. "Damn, I know you wish you coulda met her. She was a good woman and a boss in every sense of the word. Don't let nobody tell you she wasn't. Taurus was just her weakness. But that went for any female that ever met him as far as I can tell."

The doorknob shook, then it opened. A big ugly black ma'fucka with beady eyes stuck his head out the door. He looked us up and down, then pulled the door all the way open, far enough for us to see what I guessed to be Shemar sitting at a huge desk, rocking a Burberry suit. He was Caramel skinned, with green eyes. He had low cut hair into a Mohawk like style, and the top appeared to be naturally curly.

He stood up and held his hand out to Phoenix. "What's good, Cuz?"

Phoenix shook his hand, then gave him a half hug. "Mane you told me to bring him down yonder, so here he is. Taurus Junior in the flesh."

Shemar looked around Phoenix and smiled. He came and extended his hand. "Lil' homie, what it do, Potna? My name is, Shemar. Your father is the one that put me all the way in the game. I got mad love for him, as well as you and your sister. I'm sorry to hear about what you going through." He pulled me in for a half hug.

I embraced him and stood back. "I appreciate you saying that, but ain't no victims over here. That nigga finna pay for what he did and is doing to my sister. That's what brings me down here to you."

Shemar laughed and nodded his head. "Yeah, I can see that killa shit running all over you boy. You look just like yo' old man. By the way, he knew you were coming and wanted me to extend a message for him. One the I will deliver to you first thang in the morning. But right now, let's get to the bidness at hand. The head of the Cartel, Mikey, he been laying low down here in Houston, just past Cloverland. He got a nice amount of security, but these days everybody can be paid off for the right price." Shemar laughed and took a seat behind this desk. He motioned for us to have a seat on his red leather couch.

Nicki was already sitting on the edge of it. Her skirt was pulled back, both thick thighs were exposed, and glistening. I knew she was a vet and would handle her bidness if ever I was able to get between those thighs. I felt a twinge just thinking about it.

"So, what you saying, I can go and snatch this nigga up tonight, and we can end this, right now?" I was excited. I imagined having my sister back, and it made me feel giddy.

Shemar sighed. "Unfortunately, it don't work like that. Mikey got himself tied up in a few different Cartels south of the border. Cartels that are looking for him to stay alive so they can continue to pump their work into Tennessee, and the surrounding states Mikey is connected to. Long story short, his worth being alive is priced at, at least two million. If you had that in cash you would be able to drop that and be able to knock his head off right where he stood. But I doubt if that's even possible."

Nicki licked her lips. "I don't know, Shemar, after all this is Taurus's son. He might have all kinds of tricks up his sleeve." She looked into my eyes and damn near seduced me from a distance. My piece started jumping in my pants. I was thankful me and Phoenix were sitting down already.

"Well, if you do, I can make some phone calls, and we can squash this shit first thing in the morning." Shemar took a sip from a chalice that was on his desk. "Do you got bread like that?"

I shook my head. "Hell, n'all, I wish I did. That nigga Mikey was asking for a million. Had I had that kind of scratch I woulda had my sister back home already."

"Don't even trip, JaMichael. We gon' take a ride tomorrow. I promise you, by the time we come back you gon' have all of the answers, and the playbook you need in order to make shit happens trust me."

I really didn't, I didn't even know this nigga, how could I? But I nodded my head and focused my attention on Nicki's thighs. Them bitches looked real good to me. When I trailed my eyes up her sexy ass body she was looking right into my pupils, it damn near made me jump out of my skin.

"In the meantime, Shemar, ain't shit happening tonight, so I'ma spend some time with Taurus and Blaze's son so I can pick his brain a lil' bit. I know you and Phoenix got some other business y'all need to discuss. So, we'll all meet back here at nine tomorrow morning. How does that sound?" she said this looking into my eyes. My dick was jumping like crazy. I could not stop him.

"That sounds good to me. I guess I'll see you in the morning, JaMichael." Shemar shook up with JaMichael.

Phoenix stood up and gave me a half hug. "Right back here in the morning, Bruh, get some sleep."

Sleep was the last thing on my mind, and I knew Nicki had to know that.

Chapter 12

Nicki entered her condo holding my hand. She led me all the way inside and kicked the door closed. She rested her back against it, then kicked off her heels. After clapping her hands twice, her dim lights came on, followed by *Trey Songz' Jupiter Love.*

"Damn, JaMichael, your parents put together a fine young man. I can't wait to see what you look like under those clothes." She eased her Chanel jacket from her shoulders and allowed it to drop to the hardwood floor.

I stood back admiring her from a distance. She had on a skirt dress that clung to her every curve. It was so short, I could see the tops of her thighs. "How did you say you knew my parents again?"

She walked across the room all sexy like. When she got in front of me, she rubbed my chest, brought her head forward and lightly kissed my neck. "I had a thing for your father, but we never got the chance to really go there. Blaze, well, she was my babysitter when I was a lil' girl, and let's just say she taught me some thangs, I still use to this day." She licked along my neck, then flicked her tongue as if she were eating pussy it felt good.

I slid my hands around her waist and raised her skirt. As soon as her ass cheeks were exposed, I was all over them, cuffing, and squeezing. Nicki was crazy thick, I couldn't believe how perfect her body was.

"Mmm, yeah, I can tell you want some of me, boo." She spread her legs and bent forward. "Find that pussy, I dare you."

It didn't take me long. Not only did I find it, but as soon as I did, I played over the lips, and slid two fingers inside of her hot, swampy hole.

"Uuuhhh, shit, that's what I'm talking about." She slid her hand up my thighs, cuffed my piece, squeezed it through my Gucci's, and moaned again. "And I see you strapped like yo daddy. This day just keeps getting better." She stepped forward, and my fingers slipped out of her. She pushed me to the door and attacked my neck with her teeth and mouth. "I'm finna fuck yo' brains out for old time's sake. Both of your parents will be proud of me."

I didn't know if they would or not, but I damn sure was down to let her earn her stripes if that's what she was searching for. She dropped to her knees, unzipped and pulled my pants halfway down, then released my man. She squeezed him in her fist and pumped while she looked up at me with a wicked smile on her face.

"Yeah, you're most definitely Taurus's son." Her mouth was on me, taking the full length as if it were nothing more than a basic polish, but I knew better. My toes curled in my Jordan's. I had to grab onto the handle of the door for support because every sucking trick she did had me ready to buckle at the knees.

"Damn, Nicki, damn Shawty." I had to watch her in action, I couldn't take my eyes off her and came way too early. I was more embarrassed than a fat bitch sitting on a chair and breaking it.

She pumped me as fast as she could while she swallowed my cream. She even took the piece a few inches away so some of the streams could hit her tongue from a short distance. It looked sexy as hell and real Porn Star like. When she finished swallowing it all. She wiped her mouth with my piece and smiled.

"Ain't nothing short about me lil' daddy. You looking at a grown-ass woman. But don't worry, I'm finna show yo' lil' ass what it do, this Houston here, baby. We get down for the get down." She licked around the head, stood up and stepped back.

She pulled her skirt all the way up over her head. She dropped it to the floor and stood before me in a red lace Prada bra and panty set. Her titties were spilling out of the top, and her panties were stuffed with her womanly flesh. Now that she had discarded the clothes, her perfume was loud in the room. I ain't gon' even lie, looking at this grown-ass woman made me nervous. I knew my pipe game was strong, but I just figured she was 'bout that life fa real. I mean her confidence was too high. All the females I'd fucked around this time had all been my age, with the exception of Tammy. So, yeah, I was just praying I could fuck out in her bidness.

"If you see something you like come and get this shit." She walked off on her pretty toes and started her fireplace. There was a big cushion in the middle of the floor directly in front of it that seemed as if it were three feet high. She went over and sat down. "Come here lil', Taurus."

I didn't know if I liked her calling me that, but I couldn't take my eyes off those thick ass thighs. When she was walking, I noticed how her panties crept into her ass crack. It left her cheeks exposed and jiggling with each step she took. I couldn't get that image out of my head. I wanted to fuck her bad now. I pulled my shirt off and dropped it on top of her skirt dress. Next to go was my pants. I stood in front of her still in my boxers.

She rubbed the front of them and smiled. "You're a lil' heartbreaker ain't you?"

I fell to my knees and forced her thighs apart. I was done with all that verbal communicating shit. I wanted to show her how I got down. I ripped her panties off and threw them behind me. She yelped and opened her thighs wider. I smushed her sex lips together, then ran my tongue all over them, before opening them wide with my thumbs, exposing her rose-colored insides. She was dripping like a runny faucet. I attacked and went into pure beast mode, sucking that pearl like an oyster, flicking it over and over. I started talking to her while I was eating her pussy, even though my words were muffled by her dripping gap.

She grabbed the sides of my face and humped me faster and faster. "There you go, there you go, baby! Uh-uh-show me! Show me—aahhh shit!" Her thighs wound up on my shoulders, I forced her into a ball and did my thing. I loved hearing her scream and groan like she was in a state of sexual euphoria. I knew that I was causing that shit and it pushed my confidence all the way up.

She came harder, beating against the cushion. Then she pushed me off her and stood up. She looked down at me in amazement. She wiped the sweat from her forehead and squinted, looking at me as if she were trying to make sure I hadn't transformed into another person. Then she shook her head. "Okay, I got you, I got yo' ass." She ran her fingers through her cat, as the reflection from the fireplace danced over her face. She opened her lips wide again and kneeled down. Then she crawled across the floor toward me, until she was on top of me. "I'ma be yo' mama tonight. You hear me, baby? We Finna get on some real freaky shit. By the time you leave here all you gon' be able to think about is us. Trust me when I tell you this." She grabbed my piece and pulled it upward, licked over my sack and took one ball into her mouth at a time.

I was shaking, I felt her tongue travel South. She sucked right under my sack and scraped lightly with her teeth. She dropped lower, I started wondering what the fuck she was on, then her tongue disappeared up my butt.

I fell back and pushed her back a lil' bit. "Hold up, Shawty, I ain't wit' that shit."

She ran her fingers through her hair. "Nall, lil' daddy, you just need to trust me. I know what I'm doing, I got you. Now come here."

I shook my head. "Hell n'all, ain't shit going up there, Mama. I ain't ready for all that shit. Bring it back down a few notches for me."

She laughed. "Damn, yo' daddy was the same way. A'ight, I still got you. Get over here!"

I rushed her and picked her thick ass up, then flipped her on her stomach. I started eating that pussy from the back. Pulling on her lips with the ones on my face. Every time I picked my head up, I would smack her on her fat ass and dig into her sex with my two fingers at full speed. It got to the point that she rested her face on the cushion and looked back at me moaning while I fingered her at full speed for ten minutes straight. Her juices were dripping off my wrist.

"Awww, baby I'm cumming—I'm cumming. Shit, Mama cumming!" She reached under herself and diddled her jewel.

I started licking her fingers and wrist, as well as her pearl until she fell on her stomach shaking. I scooted under her, pulled her across my waist, and spanked that big 'ole ass hard. The licks were loud, every time I made contact she yelped and moaned louder. She kept her hand between her thighs and came again.

I pushed her off me and stroked my piece while she did her best to gather herself. "Come on, Mama, bring that ass over here and bend that ma'fucka over. You want some of this young dick, then back up on this ma'fucka." I removed my hand and allowed him to stick straight out.

She moaned as she got on all fours. Then she backed up and whimpered at the same time. When she finally made contact, she grabbed it, and slowly slid back on it until I was buried against her ass cheeks. "Fuck me, baby. Fuck this vet pussy. Give me that son dick." She leaned all the way forward and rested her weight on her elbows.

I grabbed her hips and pushed her forward, just to bring her back hard. Her pussy felt like a wet, hot, suction. I could feel her juices dripping off my balls, running all down my thighs. Nicki was wet, there was no doubt about that. She started working her muscles as soon as I was inside. Then I gave her the bidness as hard as I could and smacked her ass at the same time.

"Uh-uh-uh, mmm! Yes-yes, baby! Fuck—fuck, baby, oh-oh, shit," she groaned, slamming back on me.

I could feel the heat from the fireplace warming my back. After a few minutes of wrecking that cat, I began to sweat. I could taste the coke in the back of my throat. It was still dripping, and the heat seemed to boost my high all over again.

Nicki screamed and came bouncing back into me. Her juicy ass felt hot smushing into my stomach again and again. I started rubbing all over it, opening the cheeks and fingering her rosebud. It was already so slippery because of her oozing pussy.

"Yes, lil' daddy, you-want-some-of-that-fat-ass. Don't you?" She slammed back harder and harder. I was having a slightly difficult time keeping up. She was so strapped.

I flipped her ass over again, placed her back into a ball, pressed her knees to her shoulders and long stroked her. "Bitch call me, Daddy! Call me, Daddy!"

"Uh-uh, Daddy—Daddy! Fuck me, Daddy! Yes-yes, Daddy, shit daddy, I'm sorry!" She ran her tongue over her lips and tried to lean forward so she could kiss me.

I turned my head and sped up the pace. Now my pelvis was smashing into hers violently. I was beating that pussy up.

Her sex started squirting and making loud suction noises. It kept getting better and better. When I felt her hard nipples poke at my chest, I imagined pulling on them and came squirt after squirt into her thick ass.

"Uhhhh-uhhhh, yes, I feel it! Daddy, I feel it!" She kicked her legs out, and wrapped them around me tight, forcing me to go deeper into her body as I jerked, and came over and over.

When my dick became sensitive, she unwrapped her legs, and I eased from atop of her. She stood up and disappeared from the room. When she came back, she was rubbing between her cheeks.

"Ain't no way you finna leave this condo without fucking me back here. You see I was too young for yo' daddy, so that's all he would do to me is hit this ass. He the only man, I ever gave some to. I don't even fuck wit' niggas like that period, well, other than Shemar, but anyway, since you his son, it's only right you get some of this ass, too." She kneeled down and bent all the way over. "What do you say, you think you can give me five hard minutes of your time for old time's sake?"

I was behind her in seconds. She eased me into her tight back door slowly. I waited until I was halfway in and slammed him home. She yelled out, I didn't give no fuck. I started piping her like I imagined my pops used to. I knew he wouldn't have no mercy, so I didn't either. "This what you want? This what you want?"

"Yes—yes, Taurus! Lil' Taurus, yes! Aaahhh shit, Daddy! I'm cumming already!" Her right hand went crazy between her thighs.

She started shaking and I went on kill mode for ten straight minutes until I came all over her ass cheeks, and rubbed it in. Before it was all said and done, she sucked my fingers clean, and washed me up in the tub looking into my eyes the whole time, mesmerized.

Chapter 13

"Man, we been driving for a long ass time. Where the fuck are we going, Bruh?" I asked looking over at Shemar.

He pulled on his nose and leaned back in his Bentley seat. The windows were rolled up and he had a song by Pimp C blasting through the speakers. I could tell he was still down with that chopped and screwed era that made Houston famous in the nineties. I even found myself nodding my head to it.

"Lil' Bruh, fall back and enjoy the ride. Besides shouldn't you be a lil' tired? Where the fuck you getting all this energy from?"

Nicki reached from the back seat and rubbed her hand over my chest. "I'm here to tell you first-hand, lil' daddy held his own. I didn't think he had it in him."

Shemar nodded and kept rolling. "Well, anyway, we'll be there in about ten minutes. Have a lil' patience." He stepped on the gas and kept rolling.

My phone buzzed with a text from Bubbie. All it read was that she wanted me to pick up, so I did. I turned up the music so I could get a hint of privacy. "Hello?"

"Hey, Daddy, what are you doing?" she asked, sounding a bit tired.

"I'm handling bidness. What's good wit' you?"

"Well that girl, Candy's here, she saying she's ready to take Angel with her."

"A'ight, that's her daughter, so let her."

"Daddy, the thing is, she is super high, right now, and she appears drunk. She don't look like she's fit to be caring for no lil' girl, right now. So, what should I do? I didn't even let her in my house when I smelled all of that shit on her, she's waiting outside in some beat-up ass Plymouth Neon from the nineties."

"Bubbie, let that bitch in so she can get her child. Do you want her calling the police on yo' ass?"

"They wouldn't do nothing but lock her up. How the fuck she gon' drive over here all high and drunk like she is? That don't even make sense."

I saw Shemar pulling into a prison's parking lot, and my stomach muscles tensed up. "Look, Bubbie, do whatever you wanna do. I got some shit I gotta take care of down here. But my advice is give that woman her child. I'll talk to you later."

"Wait!" she hollered.

"What, Bubbie?"

"Are you with a bitch?"

"What?"

"You heard me. Are you with a bitch, right now?"

"Man, n'all, get off that dumb shit. I already told yo' ass I'm handling bidness."

Nicki busted out laughing at something Shemar said, as he was pulling into the prison's parking lot.

"Nigga, you lying. That sounds like a bitch to me, Ja-Michael. I thought you said you were out there on bidness?"

"I am, I'll holla at you when I get back. Until then you stay yo' ass in the house, and after she leaves lock them doors."

"JaMichael, tell me you love me."

Shemar turned off the radio and took his keys out of the ignition. The car was dead silent. I could tell they were waiting for me to get off the phone so they could tell me what was good. "Bubbie, do like I say, I'll be home in a couple of days."

"Daddy tell me that you love me, please."

Nicki rested her hand on my shoulder and massaged it a lil bit. "Come on, Player. We got bidness to tend, too."

I held up one finger, opened the car door, and got out. After I closed it, I got ready to tell Bubbie I loved her, but she had already hung up the phone.

***

I sat there in the plastic white chair feeling like I had gas, I was nervous and hot. I couldn't believe the prison visiting room didn't have any air condition inside of it. Nicki sat on one side of me, while Shemar decided he'd wait in the car. He feared there might have been a federal warrant out for his arrest, and he wasn't taking no chances.

"JaMichael, you gon' be good lil' daddy. Your pops was telling us he hadn't seen you since you were barely out of diapers. He finna be real happy to see you." She kissed my cheek, to comfort me.

I took another deep breath, rubbed my sweaty palms over my pants and kept looking at the door that they told me my father would walk through. I didn't know what to think or expect. I'd heard how much of a legend he really was, and part of me honored him for that. Yet, on the other hand, he was partially locked up for the brutal slayings of both me and Jahliya's mothers, though he swore that he was innocent, and would never do such a thing. I didn't know him at all. All I knew was that my heart yearned to get to know him.

Nicki squeezed my shoulder and pointed. "They finna go get yo' pops, right now."

Two guards opened the all-white metal door and disappeared inside of it. They were gon for only a few minutes, but it felt like a million years. My stomach started bubbling again. The big door clicked and next thing I knew one of the guards that had previously gone through the doors were stepping back very slow. The white metal door opened wider, then I saw him. There was Taurus, my father. He had a locked belt around his waist, along with handcuffs and shackles. His prison attire was navy blue. He had a short haircut, the waves were graying, but looked nice none the less. His muscles were bulging as if he worked out every single day tirelessly. He wore a pair of Tom Ford glasses. When our eyes locked, he smiled. His dimples were as deep as mine. I felt weak and strong at the same time. I stood up.

The guards escorted him to the glass booth that both me and Nicki were sitting in. They locked his cuffs to a steel hook under the table and stepped out of the room. "You got one hour, Stevens." Then they closed the door back loudly.

I was still standing, I didn't know what to do, or say, and my pops looked like he was equally confused. Luckily for us, Nicki was present. "Boy, if y'all don't hug I'm finna kick both of y'all asses." She promised.

I grabbed my father and I hugged him as tight as I could. I felt weak, just feeling my old man arms around me took all of that gee shit out of me if only for a few seconds. He was the only living parent I had so this embrace we shared, and his presence was extra special to me. "Damn, Pop."

He hugged me tighter. "I know son, trust me, daddy knows." He continued hugging me, we stayed that way for five full minutes. By the time we sat down we were both a little weaker, but also stronger, at least I knew that was how I felt.

"Pop, I didn't even know they were bringing me here. I was totally caught off guard. I mean, I wanted Jahliya to come, but that nigga Mikey, and them Duffle Bag niggas got her somewhere. Now some people saying my sister ain't even alive, and she all I got out there in them streets, so I'm lost." Tears came down my cheeks. I was hurting, I was missing my sister, and this was the first time I'd been in front of my father since I was old enough to remember. I felt the need to vent.

Nicki rubbed my back. "It's okay, baby. We finna figure this all out before you go back to Memphis. You can bet that shit."

106

My father Taurus nodded his head. "You damn right we is—" He paused. "Son, first of all, let me just say that as a man, I am sorry. I'm sorry for not being there for you and your sister. I'm sorry for not giving y'all a better life, and for leaving y'all the way that I did. I swear if I could change things I would in a heartbeat."

"Pops it's good, you ain't gotta apologize. All this stuff was out of your control from as far as I can see. I don't hold nothing against you. One thing I do wanna know is what happened with our mothers? Why are you sitting in here for their murders?"

He lowered his head and sat back in his chair. Then he and Nicki made eye contact.

She kissed me on the cheek and stood up. "I'll be right back, I gotta go to the bathroom." She excused herself and closed the door behind her.

Taurus waited until the coast was clear and looked over at me. "Son, I would never hurt, Blaze or Princess. Your father had a weakness for women? I couldn't be with just one, no matter how hard I tried. Women have always had a way of stealing my eyes with their physical features first, then my heart would soon follow. I'm probably the only man I know that coulda been in love with multiple women equally at one time."

I wanted to interrupt him, so I could let him know I was dealing with the same dilemma, but I wanted, no I needed him to go on so I could put to rest the doubt in my brain. I couldn't believe how much I looked just like this man. Jahliya looked just like him, too. That was scary to me.

"Son, I was crazy about Blaze. Blaze was a go-getter. A businesswoman, she was all about her paper. She saw the hustler in your father, she wanted me to expand my talents outside of the hood. She saw more in me than just a dope seller.

Princess, Jahliya's mother was a hood chick, straight from New Jersey with a past full of heartache and pain. When she and I met it was through your uncle, Juice. He and her were talking, but she didn't know at the time that Juice had killed her brother. I did, and even though I never said nothing about it, I felt responsible.

"So, I protected her, and I fell in love with her, at the same time Blaze was trying to turn me onto something new. Her vision of what life would be like outside the hood and her swag is the reason I fell in love with your mother. She represented possibilities to me. Not to mention she was one of the closest black women Texas had ever birthed. Long story short, I also had a sexual past with your grandmother, it's a long story that I'll break down at another time. It's crazy and will take a lot of explaining, but anyway, your grandmother developed strong feelings for me because I became the only unconditional love she'd ever known. When it came time for me to give up the game, and me choosing a wife for myself between either Blaze or Princess, I had difficulty.

"So, I told your grandmother to help me choose while I went out and hit one last lick that would end my career in the game. Well, she agreed to help me choose, and when I got back to my mansion in Miami it just turns out that she had chosen herself. She slayed both your mother and Princess. It's a wild story that needs to be told, but it's the truth. After I came home and found them and you and Jahliya screaming I lost my mind. Your grandmother called the police and I kept my mouth shut. What else could I do? She was my mother, I would never let her endure this shit."

I shook my head, my brain was slowly trying to process everything, and it was having a hard time. "So, grandma really did kill our mothers?"

He nodded. "Yeah, she was mentally fucked up after all she'd been through. But it was also my fault, too. I shoulda never went there with her sexually."

I lowered my head. "Damn, Pops, so are you saying that all of that stuff about our bloodline being wicked is actually true?"

"What do you mean?"

"I'm saying like our family desiring, one another? The urges for forbidden sex, betrayal and all that. Is it real?"

He thought about it for a minute. "I don't know, Son."

"Okay, so what made you go there with, Grandma? You had to have some desire for her."

"I did, for as long as I could remember. But your grand-mother was bad, Son. I don't know how she looks now, but back then she was crashing Memphis, and that was even after having a few kids."

"But Pops that was still your mother. It didn't matter how bad she was, it wasn't right."

"I know, but it happened, and I just had to let you know that." He exhaled. "So, what's up with you? Have you been going through something that made you ask me that?"

I thought about it for a minute. I wanted to tell him about the curious shit me and Jahliya had been on before Mikey snatched her up, but I couldn't look him in the eye after I told him that. I was pretty sure he still saw her as his little girl, so I decided against that. "Yeah, I done already fucked, Danyelle and went in on Veronica. It's something about that forbidden pussy that drives me crazy."

"That's your blood boy, you gotta be careful. I can't tell you how to control that monster between your legs because I never learned how to control mine. All I can say is use your common sense and strap up. Don't let too many fall in love with your sex game. Emotions and a fuck game is lethal.

That's a deadly combination for us son, trust me? It can only lead down the road of darkness, so be careful."

"Man, Pop, it's so much I wanna ask you, but I already know we ain't got the time. I know there's a reason why I'm here today, and I need to know why?"

"Well, wait, Son, before I tell you that, I gotta ask you a question."

"A'ight, go ahead."

"Your Auntie used to send me all of your writing assignments when you were in school. She even sent me some of the screenplays you wrote. I need to know if you are still interested in writing like that?"

That threw me for a loop. "Yeah, Pop, I mean whenever we get Jahliya back, and I'm able to think clearly. I would love to start writing again. Why do you ask?"

"When you leave today, I'm going to have y'all leave with a box of my manuscripts I been working on ever since I stepped foot in here. I want you to take them and finish them for me. Read them over and perfect them. All of them are true-life events, things that I been through. Your mother's story is also in there. Hers, mine and Princess'. It's labeled Raised As A Goon. It's four books, the fifth one is half done. I want you to finish it."

"Why won't you finish it, Pops?"

He shook his heads and tilted it back. Then he leaned forward. His irons made noise as he moved around. "I only got a few months before I am executed."

My heart sank. "What?"

"Yeah, six months to be exact. That's why we gotta find my baby and get her up here. Now when you leave here, I'ma have you holla at a sistah named, Shawn Walker. She and my nigga Cassius from Atlanta got a publishing company called Lock Down Publications And Cash Presents. I want you to link up with them and put our stories out there to the world. This is my one wish from you. Don't ever dumb it down or water it down. Give it to their asses just like your father wrote it. When you tell your story, you do the same thing. Do you hear me?" I nodded. "A'ight then, now that we got that out of the way. Those diamonds you have need to go to Shemar so he can open the floor for you to stank, Mikey. Mikey is being protected by more than one Mexican Cartel. They need to be paid off before we can wipe him off the map. As soon as they are paid off, we'll be able to snatch his ass up, torture him and get the information we need in order to save, Jahliya. Do you understand that?"

Nicki came and tapped on the door. Taurus waved for her to come in, and she did. She sat right beside me and rested her right hand on my thigh. "Y'all good in here, baby?"

"Yeah, we just talking about the diamonds, right now."

"Wait, how did y'all even know about the diamonds?"

Taurus laughed. "Boy, don't think that just because I'm in here, I ain't got my ear to the streets. You finna get my baby back, get her up to me, then Cash and Shawn are going to hit you with a bag for these manuscripts. Trust me on that. You'll have that diamond money back in a year's time."

"Yeah, that's cool, but how do you know Shemar's going to get Jahliya back? You're in here?"

Taurus smiled. "Son, as long as I got breath in my body, the streets are mine."

"He right about that. All I can tell you, JaMichael, is to trust your father. He has always been a man of his word. I can vouch for that, and so can Shemar."

I didn't know Shemar, or her like that, and I didn't care about either of their word, or them vouching for my father. All I wanted was my sister back. Nothing else mattered to me more than that. "A'ight, as soon as I get back to Memphis y'all can have them diamonds? To be honest with you, Pops, your books mean more to me than those stones ever could. I can't wait to read them so I can understand you and where I come from."

The guard came and beat on the door. "Time's up, Stevens!"

Me and my pops hugged, then the visit was over.

Chapter 14

An entire week had gone by and still, there had been no word from Shemar. Nicki kept me updated and told me to have faith, that it all was a process. Shemar had to do some traveling to grease palms and get the okay from certain power players. I understood to a certain degree, but I couldn't ignore my impatience. I had given them the diamonds the next day after visiting my father Taurus. I still couldn't believe I'd actually met him. I kept replaying certain parts of our visit in my head.

On the eight-day, after not hearing anything from Shemar, I found myself up at around two in the morning reading over my father's Raised As A Goon series. I was already on the second book, could not put it down. I found it crazy how he and I had the same handwriting and addressed females the same way. It seemed he had a real problem keeping his piece in his pants as much as I did. I also started to understand how the relationship developed between him and my grandmother. She was a very broken woman and Taurus had been the only one there for her after so many years of abuse, and degradation.

I became so enwrapped into the story that Bubbie was able to sneak up on me this night while I read in the basement, with a steaming cup of cappuccino. "Dang, Daddy, you been down here a long ass time. What you down here doing?" She inquired.

I was on the seventh chapter and it seemed like my Pops and my grandmother were about to finally cross that line in the book. I was thirsty to see what was going to happen next. "Nothin' baby, I'm just reading some shit I got from my father when I went to see him. Go back to bed."

She kneeled down and looked into the box. "What is all this stuff?"

I got possessive as hell real quick, as soon as I saw her touching stuff. "Bubbie, put that shit back down baby. It's sentimental to me." It was all I had from him and I didn't want nobody touching it.

She dropped the manuscript she had picked up. The title read: Rotten To The Core. I hadn't even made it that far yet. "Dang, Daddy, I'm sorry, don't bite my head off please." She rolled her eyes and struggled to get up.

I sat the manuscript down and helped her to her feet. We wound up on the couch with my arm around her. "Baby, can I ask you a question?"

She nodded. "You can, as long as you're man enough to deal with my response."

I laughed. "We gon' see."

"Gon' head and ask yo' question." She snuggled under me and placed her head against my chest. Her belly was starting to get a little bigger, but it looked good on her. Her cheeks were even chubby now.

"Bubbie, why are you so damn clingy?"

She scoffed. "I know damn well you didn't just ask me that?"

"I did, answer the question?"

She threw my arm from around her neck, stood up, pulled up her shirt and poked her stomach out. "Negro, do you see this stomach? Huh, do you? Do you see how my belly button sticking all out and shit?"

"Yeah, what about it?"

"That's why I'm so clingy. I'm clingy because you were supposed to make me a wife's before you made me a mother. But lucky for you, there is still time." She sat back down on my lap. "You got a problem with me clinging to you the way I do? Would you prefer for me to be all out in the streets fucking a bunch of different niggas while your child is grow-ing inside me? I'm talking Mexicans and all kinds of shit."

"Hell n'all, that'll get yo' ass fucked up."

"Well, that's what Tamia's doing." Bubbie smiled when she said this last part.

"What?"

"Yep, she been all on Facebook with some fine ass 'Rican nigga with a big nose. They all hugged up and kissy-kissy. Here go my phone, see for yourself."

I grabbed it out of her hand and logged on to Tamia's ac-count. The first picture I saw was of her and Chino hugged up. This made me frown. "That ain't her nigga, that's her cousin."

"Cousin my ass, you better keep on browsing."

I did just that and read all the statuses Tamia posted over their pictures. Shit about her finding her true love. About what a real man was, and how loyalty was everything. The more I read the more my understanding was fucked up. The next thing I knew I was calling her.

***

The next afternoon I waited outside of Subway until she pulled up in a black Escalade and jumped out of the truck with a Birkin bag in her left hand. She had on a tight purple and black Chanel dress, with the Gucci pumps, and two diamonds in her ear. She looked stunning and like she cost a whole lot of money. I noticed there was an all-black Benz with tinted windows parked behind her. The window rolled down, and Chino's face appeared. He was smoking on a blunt that looked fat as a green marker.

Tamia stepped past me smelling like Prada. I held the door open for her and watched how her ass jiggled under her clothes. She was putting on weight and it looked good on her as well. She went to the counter and ordered her food, then took a seat by the window. I guessed so Chino and his killas could see her. My trigger finger started itching right away. I ordered my food and took my seat across from her. She smiled and sucked juice through her straw.

"So," she started.

"So, I thought you said that 'Rican nigga was your cousin?"

"He is, but it's just by marriage. Ain't no blood running through us." She looked out the window at him and waved.

I got heated. "You think I'm finna let you fuck with that nigga over me? Don't you know how much I love yo ass, Tamia?"

"Nope, last I checked you was still living with that, Bubbie bitch. How the fuck you gon' love me when you still fuckin' wit' her?"

I ignored that question because I didn't know how to answer it. All I kept imagining was Chino fucking my baby mother. Every time I thought about it, I got so mad I was ready to kill something. "Tamia, this shit ain't happening. I been in love with you ever since I was a kid. I better be the only nigga that ever fucked still, too."

"JaMichael, who the hell do you think you are? You can't run my life and think you're going to do whatever you wanna do with your own. That's bullshit and you know it."

The worker from Subway came and put our food on the table. She sat down our chips and walked away. I didn't even look up at her. "Tamia, what do you want me to do?"

"Let me be happy, JaMichael. That's all I ask, I'm allowing you to live your life, let me do the same."

"Man, fuck that. So, what you finna do about my baby being inside of you? You keeping it?"

116

"Yeah, about that—something musta happened to Chino when he was a kid that he can't remember, but all he knows is that he can't make any children. So, he wants me to have this one. He's already put fifteen thousand up in a trust fund for our baby."

"Tamia, when you say ours you better be talking about mines, and yours."

She bit on her bottom lip. "I was." I could tell she was lying because she couldn't make eye contact with me.

That vexed me. "Bitch, now you tripping. You think you finna have a happy ass family with my seed and another nigga. You got me fucked up!"

She smiled evilly. "This what you wanted, JaMichael. You chose that bitch, so you stick with her. When the shit hit the fan, he was there for me and you weren't. You chose her. As far as you and I go, we're through. You broke my heart." She opened her food and pushed it all in my lap, then poured her drink on my head. I sat there and watched her walk outside, into Chino's arms. He looked me in the eyes one time before he ushered her back into her truck. I felt like throwing up.

***

Bubbie musta sensed something was wrong with me that night because she kept looking at me from the corners of her eyes, but she wouldn't say nothing. She had her maid whip up a platter of meatloaf and mashed potatoes. I picked over it, but I really didn't have an appetite. I dumped the food off my plate, and I went down to the basement, so I could finish reading part two to my father's Raised As A Goon series. I zoned out, kept trying to imagine what his voice sounded like in my head. On some real shit the more I read, the more I missed him, and the more I realized I came from a dysfunctional family. My uncle Juice seemed like he was out of his mind, so did my grandfather.

I was in the fifth hour of reading, and midway through his part three when Bubbie came down the stairs with her phone in her hand. She had on a sexy lil' nightgown that showed off her baby bump. She came, sat right beside me and nestled her face into my neck. "Dang, Daddy you still reading these papers?"

I was just at the end of chapter nine and finished it before I stopped. "Yeah, boo, my pops wrote all this stuff. I can't stop reading it. I see he's been through a lot. It's no wonder shit turned out like it did for our family. My grandfather was a lunatic."

She grabbed my arm and placed it between her thick thighs. Then she closed them and laid on my shoulder. "I got a confession to make."

I looked down at her. "What's that?"

"Don't get mad, but every time you leave, and I know you gon' be gone for a long time I sneak down here and read your father's books. I know I'm not supposed to, but I am having your baby, I wanna know what your true family history is. I think I deserve that. Are you mad at me?"

I shook my head. Bubbie reminded me of a little girl that was starved for her father's attention. I knew she loved me, and I was starting to feel like I needed to take it easy on her. "Nall, boo, how far have you gotten?"

"Honestly?" She looked excited to be able to admit her wrongdoings.

"Yeah."

"I'm almost done with the third part. I totally get how things transpired between him and your grandmother. I don't even see the wrong in it after reading that. It was so sad, though. I see this isn't the first time your sister Jahliya has been taken, poor baby."

I agreed. "Yeah, my family's fucked up. Aren't you worried about how our child will turn out?"

Bubbie was quiet for a second, then she started biting on her fingernails. "I guess I am a little bit, but not because of our bloodline but because of where we are with each other."

"What do you mean?"

"I mean, I don't know if we're going to be together for the long haul. Ever since you found out about, Tamia and that Chino dude your mood has been down. It's real hard for me not to notice that."

I didn't have a comeback, so I didn't even try to combat what she was saying. "You gotta understand her and I have been together since we were teenagers. She's all I really know. Then on top of that, she told me that Chino nigga was her cousin. For all, I know she coulda been fuckin' him all along."

Bubbie stood up with her cute brown belly poking out of her shirt a little bit. She ran her fingers through her hair and sighed. "Uh, I went to the obstetrician today, by myself. Ever since I found out I was pregnant with our child I've been in the house, doing all I can to show you I'm all about us having a family together. So, excuse me if I don't give a fuck about some bitch fucking around with some dude that was supposed to be her cousin. You got played. What goes around comes around." She picked up the remote control and turned on the projector, before adding a movie to it.

I sat there for a second, I had to think about what she'd just said. "What you mean what goes around comes around?"

She scoffed and laughed sarcastically. "Just like I said. Ah, you don't think I knew you was fucking, Danyelle, really Ja-Michael?" She rolled her eyes. "Nigga, I been known that from the get-go." She sat on the couch and crossed her thighs, accidentally flashing me her panties in the process.

"So, you knew, and you feel like I'm just getting what was coming to me?"

"I sure do, the Lord works in mysterious ways. You can only dish out for so long before you have to eat what you've dished out in other ways."

I sat there feeling irritated, but I knew she was right. I had been fucking Danyelle behind her back, and it's ironic that there was a possibility that Tamia was fucking Chino the whole time. Karma was a bitch like that. "What you want me to say?"

"Shit, just let that bitch go and hold me while I watch this movie. We can't change the past. The future belongs to us though, I mean at least it's supposed too."

I watched the rest of the movie in silence with her, I couldn't believe how she had a habit of playing the fool but was really always on point and knew what was going on. That quality was both sexy and extremely dangerous. After I held her until she passed out, I stayed up and wrote my first two chapters for a revised Raised as a Goon.

Chapter 15

I don't know how I let Bubbie talk me into it, but somehow, three weeks after I'd gone to visit my father, I found myself stepping onto my grandmother's porch in Baton Rouge, Louisiana. Her home was three stories high and red-bricked with a massive lawn. When we pulled up her long driveway there was a Latino guy on a riding mower getting her stuff right. To the left of him was a Spanish woman trimming the edge of my grandmother's bushes, and two men on each side of her house washing her windows. Her estate looked luxurious and comfortable. The back portion was huge, and even from where we stood in front, I could see a tennis court, and a big pool that the sun was reflecting off.

Bubbie's eyes were big. "Damn, it looks like yo' Grandma caked up. Boy, you shoulda been reached out to her."

"I didn't, you did," I snapped, walking up the steps.

"Yep, and I'm glad I did, too. Now that we've read what really happened with your parent's situation. The only way you're going to get closure is if you address all of this with her." She rang the doorbell. "Now what is her first name again?"

I shrugged my shoulders. "I don't know, I thought you knew."

"That don't make no damn sense. How do you not know your grandmother's name?" she asked, lowering her Chanel glasses.

I just pinched her lil' ass, and backed away, laughing. "That's her name."

"Ow, you ass hole." She raised her hand to slap me across the face but stopped when the door started to open.

The door swung open and I could feel my stomach turning to knots. I couldn't wait to see the fragile old woman that I imagined I'd force to tell me all our family's secrets. I wanted to hear her admit what she'd done to me and Jahliya's mothers. I didn't know what I was in for, but what I saw when she finally opened the door all the way I was not expecting.

My grandmother stood in the doorway looking beautiful. She was about five-feet-five inches and high-yellow, with hazel eyes. Her silky, curly hair fell to her waist, it was black, with a hint of gray in certain places. Her face appeared flawless as if she hadn't aged, at least I didn't think so. Her eyes were sharp, sideways and almond. Her lips were full, and her body was slim, yet, voluptuous. She wore a pair of sandals exposing her French pedicure, that matched her manicured nails. I was stunned, she didn't look a day over thirty-five.

She ignored Bubbie and looked right at me. "Oh my, God, you have to be my grandson, August?" She stepped out on to the porch to hug me.

August was the original name my father and mother named me, but when Veronica officially adopted me and Jahliya she changed it for whatever reason. "Yes, Grandma." Even though I didn't feel right doing it, I hugged her.

She seemed to melt in my arms. She hugged me tight and took a step back looking me up and down. "Taurus couldn't deny you even if he wanted, too. Look at you, you look just like his damn twin. Smile once for me, baby."

I did before I even had a chance to really smile, she stopped me. "Oh-my-God, you look just like my son. It's like I birthed you myself." She hugged me again. Her chin rested in the crux of my neck. She held me for a moment, then slowly backed off me. "And uh, who is this?"

Bubbie stepped forward and extended her hand. "How are you doing, Mrs. Stevens. My name is, Bubbie, I'm Ja-Michael's wife to be." She smiled and looked up at me.

My grandmother grabbed her left hand and turned it over. She saw there was no ring and sighed as if she were relieved. "No ring means no commitment. I don't know why women are always trying to lock my babies down." She laughed. "And please call me, Deborah. Y'all get on in this house."

Bubbie stood frozen for a second before she looked up at me. "Your grandmother ain't all there, JaMichael. I can tell something ain't right wit' that woman."

I looked into the house, my grandmother was just switching away. Her dress was all in her big booty. It was weird, yet hard to not notice that. "Look, Bubbie, you're the one that wanted me to meet her, so I could seek closure. Now we're here, you gotta deal with the crazy. It sucks to be you, right now, but let's go."

"I'm saying, did she even see my baby bump? If she did, she ain't acknowledge it. What Granny does that?"

"Apparently mine."

My grandmother came back to the door and stood there. "Okay, the first time I was asking. Now I'm telling both of y'all to get ya asses in here."

***

One thing was for sure, my grandmother could cook her ass off. She had the whole table laid out as if we were having a Thanksgiving meal. There was so much food on the table that we had to make room. Bubbie mighta been irritated by my grandmother's comments at first, but it didn't stop her from chowing down as if she were starving. She ripped the meat from her chicken bones like a savage, spooned pinto beans, white rice, and cornbread into her mouth with one hand and held her cup of fresh-squeezed lemonade with the other. She made sure she took short breaths before she stuffed her face again. Her pigging out like that was a turn on for me. I liked that she was gon' get full whether my grandmother wanted her to or not.

After we finished eating, I decided to help her with the dishes while Bubbie took a nap, after groaning about how full she was. My Grandmother dipped a plate into a bunch of soapy water, rinsed it off and handed it to me to put into the dishwater.

"Ghost, I know why you're here." She picked up another plate and started to cleanse it.

"You do?"

"You wanna know if I killed your mother, don't you?"

Damn, she caught me off guard with that question. I liked that she didn't beat around the bush. "Yeah, Grandma, I do."

"Well, baby, the answer is yes." She handed me another plate.

I was still going through the processing stage. I didn't know what I wanted to do. Most niggas would have bodied anybody that said to them what she had about my mother. But she was my grandmother, what was I supposed to do?

"Your mother had stolen, Taurus's heart. She made him become lost. He started to forget about all the things that really mattered. In addition to that, neither one of those girls were going to let him be happy. They were to head over heels for him. Whichever one he'd chosen the other would have waged war on him, or somewhere down the line, they woulda wound up hurting my baby. I couldn't allow that. Ain't no woman gon' ever love him like his mama." She washed another plate and handed it to me.

"So, why kill my mother? Why not run them off, or something else? Didn't you know I was going to be born, and need a mother? Do you have any idea how much your decision has affected me and my sister?"

She stopped and her eyes trailed upward. She shrugged her shoulders. "Honestly, baby, I didn't think that far into it. I was solely focused on making sure my son's heart was protected, and that he didn't make the wrong decision. I couldn't let those girls take him away from me. I had already lost two sons, and a daughter? How much more did the world expect me to take?"

I shook my head. She honestly had the nerve to hand me another plate as if her words had no effect on me. When I didn't load it into the dishwasher, she mugged me. "Uh, is there a problem?"

"Grandma, what is wrong with you? Do you not understand that you took two people's lives just so things could fit your agenda? You killed my mother, and it's like you're just okay with it."

"I am, that happened years ago. I got over it and you should too. Boy move out the way and let me finish this job before we be up doing this all night. I still wanna show you some VHS tapes I got of your father when Taurus was just a little boy."

I got out her way. She started humming *Mary J Blige's 'My Life'* song, as she loaded the dishwasher after washing the plates. I stood back and watched her, I could tell something was wrong, I just couldn't quite put my finger on it. When I got back into the living room Bubbie was woke, sitting up on the couch. Her eyes were low and in slits. She looked both tired and worn out. I pulled on her shirt and started to rub her belly to calm myself down. I had only been doing it for a few weeks, but I noticed that it kept me calm when I felt my anger boiling, or my anxiety going through the roof.

"Baby this lady is nuts, she just admitted to all that shit, she did to me and Jahliya's mothers, and she made it seem like it wasn't a big deal."

"*What!*" Now Bubbie was sitting all the way up. She looked over my shoulder, and down the hallway that led to the kitchen where I had come from talking to my grandmother. "Are you serious, she admitted to everything?"

I nodded. "Yep."

"Holy shit, we need to get up out of here then. That means she's crazier than we originally thought and everything your father Taurus put in his manuscripts was true. Damn, I don't feel safe now. Where is she?" Bubbie stood up and pulled her purse over her shoulder.

She had me paranoid. I stood up and felt like I had the heebee jeebees. "She in the kitchen doing the dishes."

"Cool, let's get the fuck out of here, right now." Bubbie tiptoed to the door and looked out of it.

I crept up behind her scary ass. "Arrgh!"

She jumped and damn near bumped her head on the top of the doorway before she turned around swinging like a maniac. "I hate you, JaMichael. Fuck, you always playing too much," she chastised.

I couldn't help cracking up. "Calm yo' lil' ass down. She ain't on shit. She about to show me some of my Pops tapes from when he was a shorty. I ain't leaving until I see them joints."

"Well, that's all cool and whatnot, but where I come from when a person tells you they are a murderer and have killed not just one, but three people, according to your father's books. You listen to 'em and get the hell out of Dodge. I love you, but I'm pregnant, and I'm finna wait for your ass in the car. Bye negro." She crept down the hall when she got to the end of it my Grandmother appeared with a butcher knife in her hand. "Oh my, God, we finna die!" she hollered, running to me and jumping in my arms.

My grandmother stood at the end of the hall, scratching her head. "What the hell is that girl running in my house for, Ghost? You better tell her to sit her narrow ass down before I fuck her up. You hear me?"

"Yes ma'am," I returned

"Now y'all come on downstairs to the viewing room so we can watch these tapes! Hurry up." She turned and left out of the hallway.

Bubbie got down. "JaMichael, I'm about to climb out one of these windows, I'm serious. Something ain't right wit' that one out there, Daddy, no bullshit."

I pulled her to me. "I know, baby, let's just watch these tapes, and then we out of here."

"Man, JaMichael, if this woman kills us, I swear before God, I'ma kick yo ass wherever we wind up. Now protect me, and let's go."

***

We had been watching the tapes and sitting on the couch for a full hour when my phone buzzed. I felt so stupid for putting it on the same side that Bubbie was on because she felt it right away. She tensed up and mugged me. I pulled it out and read the face. It was a message from Tamia.

Tamia: *Can you talk? It's an emergency.*

I jumped up. "Grandma, I'll be right back. I gotta answer this call it's important."

She waved me off, she was so engrossed in the television it seemed as if she didn't care what I did.

Bubbie stood up. "Who the fuck is texting you talking about it's an emergency?" she whispered.

"Baby, sit down, I'll be right back. Grandma explain to her what my father's doing in that clip," I said, leaving out the room.

Bubbie stood there seething. When I looked back over my shoulder, she was mugging me, and taking a seat back on the couch.

I got to the bathroom and Facetimed Tamia. When she came on, she was in tears, and her right eye was black. My heart sank. I became immediately overprotective of her. "Baby, what happened to you?"

She shook her head. "It's nothing, I'll be a'ight."

"A'ight my ass, who did that to you?"

She looked over her shoulder and locked the door. It looked like she was in a bathroom. "JaMichael, Chino beat me up. I got knots all over my head." She broke down crying.

"What the fuck for?"

"He dirty, JaMichael. That nigga trying to turn me out. He wants me to sell pussy for him. I can't do that, I respect myself more than that. He says I owe him for the money and cars he gave me. And now it's a bunch of his clients that are into having sex with mixed girls that are pregnant and he wanna use me. Please come get me before he forces me to. This ain't my thing, I'm so scared," she whimpered.

There was a banging on her bathroom door. "Tamia—Tamia! Mamita, open this fuckin' door before I kick it down!"

"I gotta go, JaMichael. I'm texting you the address where I'll be tomorrow night where this is supposed to happen for the first time. Please come and get me, I love you." She started texting, then the screen went black.

Bubbie came knocking on the door two minutes later, and since I had forgotten to lock it, she eased her way inside and stood with her back against it. "What's the matter, Daddy? Who was that on the phone?"

"Tamia, she's in trouble."

Bubbie moved me out of the way and left the bathroom door, slamming it closed. "Ain't nobody got time for that," she uttered and kept talking to herself as she walked down the hallway.

I sat on the toilet, trying to decide what I should do next. To say I was lost woulda been an understatement.

Ghost

Chapter 16

"JaMichael, I can't believe you finna go and save this dirty bitch? Damn, she got your nose wide open. Why you can't be like that for me?" Bubbie asked, following me around the bedroom as I got dressed. She was getting on my nerves. I knew she was jealous and that she could never see things from my perspective. I didn't have time to explain my point of view.

"Baby, this ain't gon' take that long. I'm just finna go over here and snatch her ass up. In and out, it's as simple as that." I slipped two .45s on my hip and pulled my shirt over it.

"Then what you finna do wit' her broke ass? She ain't got a pot to piss in. I know you don't think I'm about to let her come over here, so she can mooch off me? If you do you got another thang coming." She stepped into my face again preventing me from being able to grab my fatigue jacket. "Have you thought that far into it or—"

I nudged her to the side. "Shawty, you being real immature, right now. If you already know she ain't got a pot to piss in and that right now, I'm her only safe-haven since her mother put her out. Where the fuck you think she finna go?" I grabbed my coat out of the closet and made sure my black leather gloves were inside the pocket.

"Oh—my—God, Negro you done lost all your senses. You gotta be out your rabid ass mind to think I'm about to let some bitch you used to be or maybe still be in love with come and stay all up and through here? You got me fucked up. You already got yo' lil' forbidden fruit downstairs funking up my Den. What you think because my mother saying she ain't gon be back till next month sometime. You can turn this ma'fucka into yo' Playboy mansion? Boy please!"

I zipped my jacket and made sure the handles to my straps couldn't be seen. Once I confirmed they couldn't, I grabbed her and held her in my embrace.

"Let me go, JaMichael, it feels like you're squishing the baby." She tried to break free, but I could tell she wasn't using all her strength.

"Bubbie, baby, listen to me, I really need for you to hear me loud and clear. Okay?"

She broke free and crossed her arms in front of her, while she looked up at the ceiling. "What you got to say, JaMichael? Go ahead, make it good."

I held her shoulders. "Baby, I love you, and I am choosing you. I see how you riding for me and how through this whole process it's been you that's been by my side. I see that, and I love you for it. Don't get shit twisted. I'm going over here to get her because I'm supposed too. Dude taking advantage of her, and once again she got my baby inside of her. As long as she do, I gotta keep her straight. But don't let that fuck up what we got going on."

"Nall, JaMichael, don't you let that fuck up what we got going on." She snatched away from me. "Damn, I really don't want this bitch all up in my mother's house, though. Why you can't make other arrangements? Would Veronica let her stay with her?"

"I don't know, I ain't even talked to Veronica since she put Danyelle out. I guess she thinks I'm choosing sides or something, but I don't feel like getting into all of that either. For now, this is where she coming. You finna have to deal with it."

"Nall, nigga, you finna have to deal with it," she said, pointing at me. "Have you stopped to think what that's finna be like? Nigga, you finna have two pregnant bitches running around here all emotional and shit. Both vying for your love and affection. Not to mention, that lil' pretty bitch downstairs. That's three females and don't none of us get along. That's about to be as chaotic as it gets. Just think about. Nall, man, I don't know about that. This is my house, I shouldn't have to be in discomfort like that." She was back up and started pacing. "I shoulda went to Australia with my mother. When she be doing her business thing she don't ever be at the suite anyway. I coulda had some fuckin' peace and quiet." She mugged me shaking her head. "I don't even know why I love yo' ass so much anyway. You ain't even all that." She rolled her eyes and popped her head forward.

I couldn't do nothing but laugh. Sometimes when she did the girliest things it just reminded me of how young we all were. Life had a way of trying to speed up the process even when a person wasn't ready for it. Once again, I snatched her to me, this time I kissed her lips and licked them. When she moaned, I knew that I had her ass.

"Bubbie, just trust, Daddy. I got us, I'm not gon' let nothing or nobody come between us. You got my word on that. All I want you to do is try. Even if you gotta stay in this room while they're here, just try baby. Please for me?"

"You got me fucked up. You betta tell them, bitches, to stay in whatever room you finna put them in. This is my house. I'm finna move about free as a bird believe that. Get off me." She pushed me and wiped her mouth. "Gon' rescue that bitch then. I'll be here when you get back. You, betta just tell that bitch to mind her bidness when she gets here. Let her know that you and I are together, and ain't shit she can do about it. You understand that, Daddy?" She pointed two of her fingers at my temple like she was hard and shit.

I coulda snapped on her or said something else slick, but I decided against it. She was my baby and she had a right to feel how she felt. "A'ight, I ain't gon' forget that you running the show. I love you, I'll be back." I turned to leave.

She grabbed me and hugged me as tight as she could. "Please be careful, Daddy. I need you, I'd go crazy if anything happened to you."

Damn, why we have to do this. Every time I got ready to be on some killa shit? Bubbie damn near always had a way to bring me back to the mushy side. She was becoming my weakness. That's how I knew that she was meant for me. "I got this, Baby, I'll be back in a few hours."

"You promise?"

"I promise."

***

It was one o'clock in the morning, rainy, with thunder and lightning dominating the atmosphere. It was raining so hard it made it almost impossible for me to see while I was rolling, and my windshield wipers were on high. There was a strong wind coming from the south that made the storm feel tropical. I felt a cold chill go through me as I pulled my truck into the garage that was three houses down from the Tavern that Tamia was staying above. It seemed as if it was packed. There were cars lined up along the street when I drove past the Tavern just so I could check out the scenery. I didn't know what I was walking into. So, I sat there in my driver's seat and said a short prayer. After I finished, I slid on my leather gloves, opened the driver's door and jumped out into the night.

There was a ticking sound as if something had fallen from my truck when I searched the ground I saw Bubbie's little pocketknife with the pink casing. I don't know how it got inside the truck, but I didn't have time to think about it right then. I slid it into my pocket and took off jogging down the alley. The rain appeared to pick up steadier. By the time I got on the side of the Tavern my clothes were drenched, and heavy. I made my way to the side entrance and sent Tamia a text.

Three older Spanish women who smelled like heavy perfumes and alcohol walked past, looking me up and down with smiles on their wet faces. One of them, a heavyset, shorter one of the three had the nerve to reach out and grab my arm.

"Hey, Papi, what you doing tonight? You wanna have some fun?"

I laughed her off. "That sounds good, but I'm happily married."

"Oh, don't worry, your wife never has to find out. We're just visiting."

"Rosa, bring ya ass on, damn it. You're always trying to give that shit away," her buddy interjected.

"Shut up, he's cute." She unzipped her jacket and flashed me her boobs.

I had to admit they looked nice. "Still, Ma, I love my wife."

She shook her head. "Your loss then, Honey."

I was still laughing when Tamia opened the door and stepped out into the rain. "JaMichael, you came at the right time. Chino just left, he said he'll be back in thirty minutes with the dudes that he said paid him for me. He says I gotta fuck both of them."

I grabbed her wrist. "Fuck, dude, let's just book it, right now. He ain't here."

She yanked it away. "Nall, I can't do that. He ain't gon' do nothing but come find me. He already said if I ever ran away from him and he found me, he's going to kill me, and I believe him."

"You tripping, that nigga ain't about to do shit. Come on, I'll protect you." I tried to grab for her once again, but she jerked away. "Fuck is wrong wit' you man?"

"You don't know what I've been through. You don't know what I've seen him do in just a matter of days. He ain't the one to be fucked with. Trust me when I tell you that."

She wasn't doing shit but getting me geeked up. I didn't give a fuck about Chino, or what he was capable of because I knew what I was capable of. Wasn't no ho in me and wasn't no nigga that bullied females finna put fear in my heart. I was ready to smoke that nigga like a Newport Short.

"Fuck, him, let's get the fuck up out of here. We'll worry about him later. I ain't gon' tell yo' ass again."

"Okay, okay, let me go up here and grab my phone and purse. I'll be right back, matter fact, come on in." She left the door open and started making her way up the creaking stairs before I could stop her.

I followed her up them and stopped in the doorway. There were two other females sitting on the couch in stripper attire. One of them was white and appeared to be about six months pregnant. The other was a Puerto Rican and real slim, with a pregnancy belly as well. She looked to only be about three months or so. I couldn't do nothing but shake my head.

Tamia ran out of the back room with her purse and phone. "Okay, come on, we can get out of here."

"Uh-uh, where you finna go? Chino said he'd be right back and we're going to perform," the slim Puerto Rican said.

"Girl, you need to be at home. You ain't shit but fourteen. You shouldn't be performing for nobody," Tamia countered, hugging the white girl. "I'm getting out of here. Chino's crazy, and y'all should be trying to get out of here, too."

The white girl stood up. "I wanna go, I don't wanna be here either. I heard he killed two girls that he got tired of back in Chicago. He done already gave me my warning." She trailed her finger across a long scar on her neck. It looked to be about six inches long and fresh as if he had just cut her.

"What happened, right there?" I asked, stepping forward, and looking closely.

"That bitch was running her mouth too much one day, and Chino did what he was supposed to do. Bitches need to stay in line. When they get out of line it makes a pimp look bad. Even I know that" the Puerto Rican said, looking at all of us like we were the stupid ones.

"Girl, shut up, yesterday he choked your little ass out, and coulda killed you if I hadn't revived your ass. You're always making it seem like you like it here. We know you don't. You're all the way over here from Kansas, stranded. That fool done already killed your dad. So, now you're dependent on him that's all that is."

"Fuck you, Erica, you don't know nothing about me. At least I know who my baby's father is," the Puerto Rican spat.

Erica shrugged her shoulders. "And, where does that get you? Chino don't give no fuck about you or that baby. So, who cares if he's the father, Jessie?"

Jessie lowered her head and got lost in her own thoughts. "You know what, fuck this. I'm calling him, right now." She pulled out her phone and proceeded to text.

Erica grabbed it and threw it against the wall as hard as she could. It ricocheted but didn't break like I thought it would. "Fuck, stop being so stupid!" she hollered.

Jessie stood up and lowered her head. The next thing I knew she was running at Ericka, swinging with her head down. They collided and fell back in a wrestling battle, shattering the glass table. They were making so much noise I had to stop them. Tamia started grabbing Jessie while I went for a kicking Erica. We were so engrossed in breaking up the fight we didn't even hear Chino creep up the stairs.

"So, what the fuck is going on here?" he snapped.

Chapter 17

I jumped up and for the first time, he and I made eye contact. "Chino, I—"

"What the fuck are you doing here? Tamia, what the fuck is he doing here?" Chino asked, pointing at me.

"Chino, I needed him to bring me my uh, my uh—"

"She was going to run away with him and so was this bitch, Erica. They were talking some dirty shit about you, Chino and they tried to jump me," Jessie said, getting up standing beside him. "I was sending you a text to tell you what was going on and they all tried to stop me. That's how my phone got broke."

Chino raised his hand and back slapped her so hard she flew into the wall and was knocked out. "You shoulda text me earlier," he said, calmly. "Where the fuck does your loyalties lie?" Tamia hid behind me. "As far as you muthafuckas go, you bitches are getting back to work. You, JaMichael, young' get the fuck out of my pussy trap. These hoes got clients on the way. You can't be here when they come." He opened the door and stepped to the side.

"I thought she was your cousin. This how you do your, family? You gon' make her sell pussy while she's with child, seriously?"

"This don't got shit to do with you. She dropped yo black ass for me. Now step, before I beat you like I beat these hoes. This is your last warning." He went under his shirt and cocked his .9 millimeter.

I looked down at it and nodded, sucking my teeth in defeat. "Yeah, a'ight nigga, you got it." I turned to Tamia. "Look, Ma, I guess you finna have to fuck wit' dude now. You made your choice and it ain't for me to stand in the way of the decision you made. I do love you, though." I hugged her and broke our embrace quick.

"But, JaMichael, he gon beat me black and blue when you leave. Please don't do this, please," Tamia begged.

"Tamia, it ain't my bidness no more. I'm sorry, I gotta go." She grabbed ahold of me. "Please don't do this. Please, he's gon' kill me, JaMichael."

"Get off me man." I broke her grip and nudged her off me. "Bitch you belong to him now."

Chino walked over and grabbed her by the throat. "You snake ass bitch. You heard what he said." He smacked her with the gun and flung her against the wall. She crashed into it and fell on her ass with blood leaking down to her chin. She looked helpless.

My eyes got big as planets then I snapped. I rushed Chino with blazing speed. Before he could even raise his arm to fire his weapon, he felt five of my hardest blows, all face shots. *Right! Left! Right! Right! Uppercut!*

He flew into the wall as she'd done. His gun slid across the floor. He sat there for a moment knocked dizzy. His face began to swell right away. "Fuck is wrong wit' you, nigga? You don't be hitting no female wit' a pistol."

Jessie ran, picked up the gun and aimed it at me. "I'll kill you, you black bastard. How dare you put your hands on, Chino like that?" She still had blood leaking from the corners of her mouth from where Chino had slapped her silly.

Tamia slowly rose to her feet. She eased along the wall, reached and grabbed something from my pocket. I felt her go in it. "Don't do this, Jessie. He was only protecting us. Chino, don't give a fuck whether we live or die."

Chino slowly struggled to get to his feet. "That's a lie, Mamita. I love you, Bitch. Now shoot him, shoot that nigga dead," he ordered.

Jessie held the gun straight out and squeezed the trigger over and over, looking to follow Chino's orders. It wouldn't fire, she tried harder, biting into her lip, still nothing.

Chino rushed me. "Take it off safety, flip the switch!"

"Oh, yeah, I forgot Chino, I'm sorry!" Jessie yelled, turning the gun sideways, to follow his directives.

Chino tackled me into the China cabinet, and it shattered. Shards of glass popped into the air and went all over the room. A shot fired, Tamia tackled Jessie and Erica ran out of the room. I was able to flip Chino over with ease, then I was plowing him with blow after blow, back to back, until my knuckles felt like they were too swollen to punch anymore. I stood up and looked down at him. His mouth hung wide open. His eyes were closed, his breathing was ragged and heavy.

"Fuck nigga, get yo ass up."

He scooted back, his face looked lumpy. It was caked with blood. Three of his teeth were missing. He used the wall to come to his feet. He staggered from side to side. "You shoulda kilt me, JaMichael. Don't you know who the fuck I am?" He spat and a thick rope of blood stuck to the side of his chin.

I glanced to my left Tamia was slowly standing with the gun in her hand. Jessie lay on the floor not moving, I couldn't understand why that was. Tamia aimed the gun at Chino. "You played me, Chino. I thought you cared about me. I thought you loved me, but you played me. You played me for a fool."

Chino staggered and looked over at her. "Bitch, ain't nothing free in this world. I don't give a fuck if you're my cousin or not. You gon' pay me what you owe me, or you gon' lose your life. Bitch, I'm Chino, Westside Yack. You think I'm worried about you shooting me? I made you!" He rushed her.

I shook my head and stood back. "Hit 'em, Tamia, now!"

Bocka! Bocka! Bocka! The holes filled Chino, but he still managed to make it to her. He wrapped his hands around her neck, and she popped him two more times. Smoke emitted from his back after the two holes appeared. He fell off her on to his forehead.

Tamia lowered the smoking gun. She dropped it and fell to her knees beside Jessie? When she rolled Jessie to her back, I was able to see Bubbie's pocketknife sticking out of her neck. "Fuck, Jessie, you made me do it. You made me do this. I didn't want to. Lord, knows I didn't."

I heard sirens in the far distance. "Tamia, we gotta get out of here, come on."

"No, JaMichael, look, I killed her—she's dead. Oh my, God, how am I going to live with myself?"

"Tamia, fuck her. We gotta go if we don't we finna go to jail."

That seemed to snap her out of her daze. She stood up and ran over to me drunk like. "I'm sorry, JaMichael. I shoulda never chose him over you. Please forgive me! I don't wanna fight no more."

I grabbed her hand and rushed over to Jessie. I grabbed Bubbie's pocket knife out of her neck. A rush of blood spilled out of her, onto her shoulder blade. I picked up Chino's pistol and we bounced with Tamia crying beside me the entire time.

***

Tamia paced back and forth in front of me two hours later inside Bubbie's spare bedroom. She was fresh out of the shower, but she still looked worn down. Her face was slowly beginning to heal, but the scars were still present. "Damn, she still ain't answered my texts. I pray to God she ain't gone to the police," she said, shaking her head.

"Man, you, stressing yourself out over nothing. You can't change whatever, Erica's about to do. We just gon have to fight that shit head-on when it happens. Ain't nothing we can do about it, right now."

Tamia kept pacing. "But you know I ain't do that on purpose right, JaMichael? I mean why would I just kill her for nothing? That ain't even my thing."

I stood up and blocked her path. I allowed her to walk into my arms. I held her. "Tamia, calm down. You need to get some rest. At least for a few hours. All this stressing can't be good for the baby."

"Damn, the baby right now, JaMichael. What about me? All this stressing can't be good for me, in fact, I know it ain't. I feel like I'm losing my mind." She broke away from me and sat on the bed.

I was on her again, I sat beside her and put my arm around her shoulder. "Look, I'm not about to leave your side. We're in this shit together. Now we'll figure things out in the morning. You need to get a good night's rest."

She sighed. "How can I sleep, JaMichael, when I'm in your bitch's house, and all of this stuff done taken place? How do she feel about me staying here, anyway?"

Bubbie stuck her head into the room. "Oh, it's simple, I don't want you or your drama here, but my man convinced me that you ain't got nobody else to depend on, and nowhere to go. So, you gotta stay here for a few days. I was hoping you went to a homeless shelter. I'm just saying." Bubbie walked over and pulled my arm from around Tamia. "That's doing too much."

I frowned. "Damn, Bubbie, don't start this bullshit. I already told you what I gotta do. Now take yo ass back downstairs."

Bubbie jerked her head back and placed her open hand on her chest. "Excuse you! Who the fuck are you talking too like that, especially in front of this bitch?"

"Look, Bubbie, I know I gotta stay in your house and all, but I ain't gon' be too many more of your bitches. Now I'm trying to be nice."

"Ah, so this is you trying to be nice? You kick my man to the curb for that smooth, talking Puerto Rican nigga. He winds up putting you out on the track, and you expect, JaMichael, to come save yo' ass. Now you think he finna be your knight in shining armor. You got the game all the way fucked up. You can stay here for one week, bitch. A week is all you getting. JaMichael, in the hallway, now!" She stomped her feet, all the way until she got outside the door and stood there with her arms crossed.

Tamia shook her head. "Gone head, JaMichael, before she tries to put me out tonight. I'm finna do all I can to make other arrangements before we get anywhere close to that week running out."

"Please do, uh, JaMichael, let's go."

I hugged Tamia. "I'll holler at you in the morning. Try yo' best to get some sleep."

"I will, goodnight, and thank you for rescuing me. I knew you would."

"JaMichael, let's go!" Bubbie hollered.

***

When we made it to the room that she and I slept in Bubbie was the shade of red. She had both of her fists balled up, with her stomach poking out of her shirt. "You-have-got-to-be-fuckin'-kidding-me!"

I took off my shirt and threw it in the hamper. Then off came the white tank-top. "Man, why the fuck are you so immature?"

"I'm immature, me, are you fuckin serious? You got some bitch downstairs that's in love with you, staying in my house. She dumped yo' ass for a whole other man, and you take yo sucka for love ass out here to go rescue her, giving her even more reasons to be head over heels. Now you think it's cool for all of us to mingle under one roof, but I'm supposed to be the one too feeble-minded, or immature to see what's taking place right before my fucking eyes. Man, kiss my ass, Ja-Michael. You're playing a dirty ass game and my stupid ass is allowing you to get away with it. You ain't even that slick. I don't know why I keep letting you shit on me? Sooner or later I'm gon' be scorned, and you gon' get everything you got coming, believe that Potna." She walked over and closed the door, locking it.

"Why you lock it?"

"Cause I don't trust that bitch and I don't trust you that's why. You ain't taking your ass back outside this room tonight either. You're stuck in here with me so deal wit' it. I'll be damn if y'all fuck on my watch. You're a hero, right now too, boy that'll be some of the best sex in the world I bet." She scoffed.

I stood watching her as she pulled back the blankets and prepared for us to slip into bed. I ain't even feel like arguing. I just finished taking off my clothes, climbed in bed beside her and pulled her to me. My face rested inside of her hair. "Your lil' ass don't be giving me no room to breathe. Do you know that?"

She cut off the lamp. "How the fuck I ain't giving you no room to breathe? You got two other bitches in this house that you're fuckin'. Ma'fuckas wit' asthma wished they could breathe as freely as you."

I laughed at that. "Yeah, well, you see which bed I'm sleeping in, though?"

"That don't mean nothin'. I gotta go to sleep eventually, and you know I'm a hard sleeper. I'll tell you what, though, I bet not wake up and catch you fuckin' either one of them hoes. If I do, we gon' have a serious problem. I promise you that. Oh, yeah, you definitely finna come wit' me to visit my great grandmother in the nursing home tomorrow. I went with you to see yours, and she stayed all the way out in Baton Rouge, Louisiana."

"Bubbie, I'm not going to no nursing home. I gotta lay low for a few days. That shit me and Tamia did was hot. It's guaranteed to be all over the news for the next few days."

She sat up. "Dang, y'all had to do something like that? Are you serious?"

I nodded. "Lay back down, I was just getting comfortable."

She laid back on her side and snuggled under me. "You always getting in some bullshit. Daddy, you gon have to get all that shit out of your system before our baby is born. We ain't finna raise no dysfunctional child like your father was, shit, or you. You know we find out the sex in two weeks? Do you wanna know what we're having?"

"Yeah, long as it's a girl."

"Why you want a girl? You got a girl, right here. You ain't even taking care of me," she grunted.

"Yeah, well, she gon be straight. I don't think she gon be getting on my nerves as much as you do. That's why I ain't gon' have no problem loving her like crazy."

She sat up and popped me on the leg. "That's not nice. You're supposed to love me no matter if I get on yo damn nerves or not."

I hugged her and placed her ass in my lap. "I was just playing. You know I love you, boo. Now come on, let's get some sleep."

We snuggled together and it was quiet for a moment. I could hear the crickets chirping outside, it got me lost in thought. I started thinking about Jahliya, then my father and lastly the situation I'd walked into with Tamia. My head started spinning, the silence was too much until she broke it.

"Daddy, you still woke?"

"Yep."

"Can I ask you a question and I want you to give me an honest answer, too? I don't want you running game on me, not that you got any anyway, but still."

"Gon' head ask away, Bubbie." I cuddled closer to her and rubbed our baby bump. It felt hot and kind of hard.

"We're supposed to have this baby in about five months. I need to know if you'll be able to do the right thing before then?"

"What do you mean?"

"I already told you, I never wanted to become a mother before I became a wife. You need to step yo' game up and make me a wife, I'm serious. Our child needs to come into this world the right way. So, my question is do you think you'll be able to do the right thing before then?"

"I don't know, Bubbie. We young as hell. You really can see us getting married while we're this age?"

"You really saw yourself screwing me while we were this young, so why not?"

"Touché on that. Well, baby, I don't know. I think you'll definitely make a good wife. I know I could see myself falling more and more—"

"Goodnight, JaMichael, I'll see you in the morning. I don't wanna hear that game shit, boy night, night." She elbowed me so that I got off her and pulled the blanket over her head. "I ain't gon' wait around for you forever."

I laid there until the wee hours of the night going over everything she'd asked and said. I knew she had a point. A man should never make a woman a mother before he made her a wife. As the mother to my child she deserved to be my wife, it was just the immature part of me playing devil's advocate. It was saying Tamia was also pregnant, so did that mean that she shoulda had the right to be my wife as well? I finally went to sleep with a migraine.

Chapter 18

The next morning, I was freshly showered and putting a lil' baby powder on my chest when somebody knocked twice, then opened the bedroom door and Danyelle stuck her head in. "Sup, cuz, where your evil ass baby mama?" She smiled and looked me over with her hazel eyes.

"She had to drive downstate to visit her Nana in a nursing home." I rubbed on some deodorant, slid my black tank-top over my head, sprayed some Polo cologne in my hands, and rubbed my waves with it.

"That's where she dragged Tamia off too, damn she petty as hell. She wanted to make sure y'all ain't getting down behind her back," Danyelle said stepping into the room.

"Nall, Tamia asked if she could go with her. She said they needed to talk so they could get an understanding and I agreed." I put my Polo socks on, then the shorts.

"Why you doing all that?" she asked, frowning.

"All what?"

She pulled her nightgown over her head and stood before me in just her bikini panties. "You already know what time it is. We ain't fucked in how long?" She came over and rubbed my front.

I knocked her hand away. "Get yo' ass off me."

"What's the matter with you?" Her eyebrows furrowed.

"We ain't finna fuck where, Bubbie, lay her head. That'll be bogus as hell."

"Dang, my bad I wasn't even thinking. I just want some of you cuz. I need you to fuck me before they get back." She slid her hand into her panties.

I could see the fingers moving around on the other side of the material. My dick started getting hard, but I was trying to think about the conversation I'd had with Bubbie the night before. I felt like I needed to start getting better control over my dick, or it was going to be a problem for us.

"Nall, I ain't fuckin' wit' you. I gotta start holding, Shawty down the right way. I can't keep fuckin' a bunch of different bitches that ain't cool."

Danyelle looked stunned. "You ain't, you just giving me some of this from time to time. Damn, why would you take my virginity like that if you didn't want me to be all over you all the time?" she whined. "I need you." She rubbed her panty covered pussy against my thigh and her fingers under my nose.

As soon as I smelled that pussy my dick got super hard. That forbidden part of me started to take over. I started getting hot. My vision got cloudy for a minute and my heartbeat sped up. I grabbed her and gripped that ass. Her cheeks were heavy, and hot in my hands. "Why you keep tempting me lil cuz? You see I'm tryna do right."

She kissed my lips and grabbed the back of my head. In one jump, her legs were wrapped around me, and I was carrying her into the next bedroom, where I held her against the wall and dropped my clothes. Her panties were pulled to the side, and she was bouncing up and down at full speed, while I got deep into her pussy. Ten strokes and she was already cumming, digging her nails into my shoulders.

"Uh-uh-uh, Cuz! Uh, baby, yes-yes-yes!" she moaned bouncing up and down.

She was internally hot and leaking more than I remembered. I started grunting and piping her down. We wound up on the floor as I went full boar, with no mercy. "Uh-uh-uh, shit-uh-uh—uh!"

"Yes—yes, JaMichael! JaMichael, I'm cumming! I'm cumming again, cuz, aw fuck!" She started shaking with all her might, while she held onto me.

My ass cocked back, only to slam forward, stroking at full speed. I already had my mind made up that it would be the last time I fucked her, so I wanted to enjoy it. When her toes touched my ears on both sides because her ankles were on my shoulders, I hollered out and came deep inside her, over and over. I even pulled him out and milked all over her stomach, and breasts. Her nipples stood up like pencil erasers as she rubbed it into her skin.

She reached, pulled my piece to her, and sucked the juices off it. I kept fingering her cat and enjoying the feel of it. Then she spit me out and her eyes got big as pizza pans. "JaMichael, watch out!"

I felt something hard hit me on the back of the head. I fell backward and jumped up naked! Blood rushed out of my wound and down my back. I turned around to see Bubbie holding a broom in her hand. "You dirty muthafucka, I knew you was screwing this bitch! I just knew it!" She raised it to swing again.

I noticed Tamia standing by the door with her mouth covered. She shook her head, I felt so embarrassed. Before the next blow could rain down on me, I blocked it with my forearm and the broom broke.

"I hate you!" she screamed, then dropped the broom and ran at a naked Danyelle. I could see her love juice still running down her thighs.

Danyelle threw up her guard. "Bubbie, you're pregnant. This ain't what you want. I'm sorry!"

Bubbie wasn't trying to hear none of that. She started swinging wildly and connected three times before Danyelle started swinging back. She hit Bubbie twice knocking her on the bed. Bubbie bounced right back up and went at her again. This time she was swinging even harder than before. She rocked Danyelle twice in the face and pulled her long hair, slinging her to the ground. Then she was on top of her fucking her up.

"You, ungrateful bitch! How dare you. How dare you take advantage of me?" More blows rained down.

I could feel the blood pouring down my neck. I grabbed Bubbie off her and carried her all the way to the bedroom that she and I slept in. I sat her on the bed and ran to close the door. She was up and at me right away. She hit me right in the jaw, dazing me. Then she jumped on my back and bit me on top of the head. I actually felt her teeth sink into me. It stung like a muthafucka.

I backed up to the bed again and peeled her off me. She wound up halfway in the bed. "I want you out of my house, JaMichael, tonight! Get yo' shit and take yo punk ass cousin wit' you! I hope I never see yo' trifling ass again, I hate you!" She picked up the lamp and tossed it at me.

It crashed by the door. She looked around for something else to throw. When she couldn't find anything she knew would hurt me, she crazily tried to pick up the dresser for some reason. "I'm so *ang—ry*!" she screamed, then passed out.

***

Because that shit me and Tamia did was all over the news, I wound up driving Bubbie two hours outside of Memphis to the hospital. I told them I was the father of her child and that she'd been doing some basic chores around the house when she fainted. They admitted her and placed her on fluids to hydrate her body right away. The doctor saw her and said her blood pressure had been way too high and she was lucky because any higher she coulda had a stroke. I'd gotten her to the hospital just in time. He told me I shoulda been proud of myself.

Well, I wasn't I felt like shit. I had betrayed and failed her again. I knew something was wrong with me. This is when I started to believe I was fucked up. The doctor gave Bubbie a sedative that he said would keep her out for at least eight hours. I intended on being by her side the entire time. I felt it was the least I could do. I took my laptop and for the next six hours while she slept I sat there and started writing my life's story since my father had labeled his Raised As A Goon, I figured I'd label mine Heartless Goon. Those hours flew by because I disappeared into the pages. By the time daybreak came around, I was already on chapter five, and I wanted to keep going.

Bubbie moved, then groaned. She stretched her legs and hands. When her eyes opened, and she saw me she frowned. "What are you doing here, JaMichael, and where am I?"

"Shawty, chill, you in the hospital. The doctors said your blood pressure was through the roof. You collapsed and was seconds away from having a stroke."

"If I'd had one you would have been the cause. I can't believe you would fuck that bitch behind my back. Less than eight hours after we had our talk. Damn, I can't stand you." She sat back on her pillow and looked up at the ceiling.

I was speechless. What could I have possibly said? I couldn't apologize, she knew I wouldn't have meant it. I mean, it was like she said, we had just finished talking about it, and I had gone and did the goofy.

She sat up and looked over at me disgusted. "Damn, ain't you gon' say nothin'? What you ain't got no weak-ass game to come at me with?"

I stepped toward her bed and stopped when my phone buzzed. I looked down at the text.

Shemar: *Kid, we found Jahliya. We riding out to get her tonight. I'm on my way to Memphis to scoop you, I'm six hours out.*

"Who the fuck is that, is it Tamia? Nall, my bad or is it, Danyelle?" She waited for a second. "It don't matter who it is because it's supposed to be all about me, right now!" she hollered. Her monitors started beeping and going crazy. I looked and saw that her heart rate was through the roof. I hurried to her side.

The nurse rushed into the room and checked her monitors. She placed her hand on Bubbie's shoulder. "Are you okay, baby?"

Bubbie nodded. "I just need to talk to him alone. I'm emotional, thank you."

"You bet." The nurse smiled, at me and closed the door.

I was sick, I knew I had to say something, even if she didn't buy my bullshit. I took a deep breath. "Baby, I'm sorry. That was Shemar, he said they found my sister. Baby, all of this will be over after tonight. They found her."

Bubbie kept silent, she closed her eyes for a full minute, next thing I knew she was crying? Her monitors continued to beep. "JaMichael, I'm too young for this," her voice cracked up.

"Too young for what, baby?"

"For the shit, I am going through with you. I love you, but you are killing me."

I took hold of her hand and kissed the back of it. "Bubbie, I swear to God I'm sorry. Baby, there is something wrong with me."

"Yeah, I know, and until you figure out what it is, I gotta let you go, JaMichael. I'm sorry, I already know when your sister comes home it's a wrap for us anyway. You won't have time for me. But before you leave, have you ever asked yourself why I love you so hard even though you be fuckin' me over like crazy?"

I nodded. "Yeah, I have, I just couldn't ask you no shit like that, but I would like to know. Are you gon' tell me?"

She sat up in her bed. "It's because my father never gave two fucks about me. My whole life all I ever wanted was his love and attention, but he insisted on running the streets and keeping me on the back burner. He never spent time with me or told me I was beautiful. He never instilled in me my worth. I don't understand why I love you so much because you are a spitting image of him, both in ways, and likeness. All I ever wanted was your love, that's it." Tears ran down her face. She laid back on the pillow with her eyes open, looking at the ceiling. "Leave, JaMichael, please. I just need some time to think. The doctors are keeping me here for forty-eight hours. I don't want to see you until then.

"Baby, I—"

"Just go, please don't say another word."

I didn't.

Ghost

Chapter 19

"A'ight, JaMichael, you remember what I said about that fool being connected to some major dudes, right?"

I nodded. "Yeah, you talking about ma'fuckas south of the border right?"

"Right, anyway, it wasn't easy getting them to give him up. I ran into a few problems, that's why it took so long. You see this shit ain't the movies. You can't just run up on, Mikey and waste him. Mikey is a walking investment to a lot of dangerous and important people. When it comes to the game, any time you dealing with bosses you have to understand they represent a whole army of ma'fuckas under them. An army that's looking to put food on their tables by payment from that boss. But every boss is under another boss. The streets got checks and balances just like the government. Everybody gotta answer to somebody, that way can't no one man get too big for his britches. You feel me?"

I did so I nodded. "So, how was we able to get the go ahead to handle him?"

"Well, like I said before, Mikey had a proper place in the slums. He is what you would call a flooder or a supplier to the city of Memphis, particularly all through Black Haven, and Orange Mound where our people are. The only way I was able to get the go ahead to get rid of him was because I told them he could be replaced by another more trustworthy and loyal kingpin with royal ties to the streets."

"That's what's up. You ain't gon' have no problem finding them somebody like that, right?" I asked taking a sip from the bottle of Pepsi that Shemar had given me.

"Nall, Kid, I ain't because I already found him. He gon' be working directly under me. So, it's all good."

"Cool, so when do we hit up, Mikey?"

Shemar kept rolling down the highway. It was a bit congested because it was so early in the morning. "JaMichael, you the ma'fucka that we talking about replacing Mikey with. You got royal ties. Your pops though he locked up still got connections all over the South and on the islands. As long as you keep shit on the up and up you can live real good."

"Nall, not me. I just want my sister back. Fuck the game. I ain't been doing nothing but losing in it ever since I jumped off the porch. I just wanna get Jahliya back, then I'm taking my ass to college. I'ma do the movie thang. I got dreams that extend out of the hood. The game ain't for me if it's one thing my Pop's books showed me it was that."

Shemar switched lanes in his Maybach. The interior was lit up like a spaceship. He had two televisions in each headrest, and one in the dashboard that was playing a movie with Kevin Hart. "Damn, I fucked up and allowed you to think you had a choice. We talking about the muthafuckin' Mexican Cartel. Them savages don't give a fuck about you or me, and they definitely don't give a fuck about Jahliya's life. After I gave them those diamonds, they looked at me like I was crazy. That was peanuts to them. They expected Mikey to move five hundred million in Tar by the end of the summer. All we paid them was three million in jewels. The ma'fucka that I made the deal with probably put that ice on his side bitch's finger. That's how petty it was to them. It's a life for a life. We take Mikey's, and his position dies with it. But we replace his life and his position with yours. Only you can be Jahliya's sacrifice. That's how the game goes."

We rolled in silence for what seemed like a long time. All I kept imagining was seeing my sister again. I wanted to hold her, I wanted to watch her eat. I wanted to see her smile, I wanted to hear her laugh. I was thirsty to see her eyes blink. If I had to be her sacrifice, then it was what it was. I would do anything for her, she was my world. "You know what, She-mar, fuck it. I'll do whatever I gotta do to get my sister home safe and sound. As long as I can hold her in my arms again that's all that matters."

Shemar smiled faintly. "I hear that that's how I was about my sister, Purity." He kept rolling.

Some females in a blue Benz honked their horn at his car. The driver rolled her window down and waved for him to pull over. She looked Mexican, she had on a lil' too much make up for my taste, but she appeared bad none the less.

Instead of pulling over, Shemar stepped on the gas and the car shot off like a rocket. He switched gears and punched it again. His speed reached a hunnit and ten. "Fuck them, bitches, we on something." He switched lanes five times at full speed before he slowed down.

The police detector on the dashboard clicked, then beeped indicating there was a trooper somewhere close by. Shemar eased on the brake and kept the car rolling at an even seventy miles an hour. Sure enough, we passed a Trooper on the side of the road. Shemar laughed and kept it moving.

"You said used, too. What happened to your sister, Purity?" I asked, twisting the cap back on my drink.

He shook his head. "She passed away, a lil' while ago, but it's good. I'm finally managing to get over it."

"I'm sorry to hear that, big homie. I can only imagine the pain you went through."

"Like I said, I'm finally coming to grips with it. Let's focus on the task at hand. So, before we go at Mikey's chin there are two things you need to know. The first thing is, I'm taking you right now so you can shake the hand of, Jefe' Pablo. He is the boss of the bosses for the Cold Heart Cartel. He's the one that approved for Mikey to be replaced and deadened.

Number two, we know where Jahliya is, but we don't know if she's alive, and well."

"Wait." My heart dropped. "What is that supposed to mean?"

"It means just what I said, JaMichael. You see Mikey is holding her ass in one of the cellars in the fifth ward out here in Houston. Right off Liberty Street. I got the four one-one, on all that, but I don't know her state. If I did I woulda never brought this part up. I just gotta keep shit one hunnit with you all the way around the board."

I sat there looking stupid as it began to rain again. "How the fuck you know everything else, but you don't know if she's alive or not? Fuck this shit sucks."

"Yeah, I know."

"Wait a minute, you saying, I gotta meet up with dude first to shake his hand? Don't the shaking of a hand in the Cartel world mean I'm agreeing to something, or I'm lying in bed with whoever the person's hand I'm shaking?"

"It's even deeper than that. In this case, it means you are giving, Jefe' Pablo your life, and only he's in charge of whether you live or die. It's deep kid."

"And you saying even if my sister ain't okay, I still gotta agree to this setup?"

"Unfortunately."

"Who's to say they don't already know she ain't alive? That's if all this shit ain't a scam?"

"It might be," Shemar admitted. "So, what you wanna do?"

***

We'd been traveling through the woods for damn near fifteen minutes. Not only was I worried about where the fuck we were going, but I couldn't get the thought of something happening to Jahliya out of my mind. I just didn't understand how Shemar could say he knew where she was, but he didn't know for sure if she was alive or dead. It all seemed fishy to me. I started thinking he mighta been involved with something that had something to do with my father, and this whole thing was actually bigger than me. My mind started playing all kinds of tricks on me. Especially since it had been so long since I'd seen anything other than trees.

"Damn, nigga, how much longer we gotta fuck around in these woods? I'm seeing all kinds of weird-ass animals and shit."

Shemar just kept rolling. "That's how these Cartel muthafuckas roll. They are real secretive. We just gotta follow their way of doing things. And you better get used to it seeming as Pablo planning on you being under him for a long time." He stepped on the gas and kicked up dirt.

About fifteen miles outside of Houston he switched whips. Now we were rolling a Dodge Durango with New Mexico plates on them. Shemar said the truck had been ordered for us to drive by Pablo. As far as I could tell Shemar was nothing more than a lackey. He seemed to be terrified of this Pablo dude. I didn't know him, and already hated him and his Cartel. I could never be like Shemar, I didn't give a fuck what was at stake.

After rolling for twenty-plus minutes, finally, Shemar flew out of the woods and sped beside a long creek. I saw the red eyes of Alligators lighting up in the night. They looked huge to me. The next thing I knew we were rolling right alongside the creek. So close that water was splashing up on my window. He dodged more than one alligator and kept speeding.

"Why the fuck we so close to this water? Don't you see all of them Alligators?"

He turned up *Moneybagg Yo* album and kept right on speeding. One Alligator seemed to come out of nowhere. He swerved around it and the truck fishtailed for a few feet before he straightened it back out. Then he was zooming again. Now I was feeling uncomfortable in my seat. I didn't know what the fuck was going on, but him ignoring me sent my anxiety through the roof. I started to look and check out my surroundings. There was nothing but water and pairs upon pairs of red eyes. It even smelled like a swamp. Shemar kicked up more water. My whole entire window turned a murky green.

I didn't know if I was tripping or not, but it seemed like he kept in getting closer, and closer into the water.

"Shemar, what are you doing?" He ignored me.

Now the truck was actually treading water. He cut the engine and took the keys out. Then he reached into the back seat and grabbed two paddles that were on the floor. I didn't even know they were there.

He handed me one. "Come on, we got a little work to do.

"What?"

"You heard me, Shawty. You see that boat, right there?" He pointed and flicked the lights on high beams?

I was able to see a flimsy weak ass looking boat. Around it were the tails of six Alligators. At least I thought they were Alligators.

"Bruh, you mean to tell me we gotta go out into this fucking swamp with a million Alligators swimming around in it?"

"Yep, that's how the Cartel roll. We can't do shit about it. You wanna bring Jahliya home, right?"

"Of, course, I do."

"Then you about to get into this water, and we finna paddle that boat, right there." He pointed at the boat again.

One of the Alligators slammed his tail into the water and created a big splash. I was scared as a muthafucka. I was literally shaking, I had to think about Jahliya. I would do anything for her. "A'ight, Shemar, let's go."

He pushed open his driver's door and eased into the water. I was right behind him. The water smelled like spoiled broccoli and felt cold as frozen water. There seemed to be a million bugs out and all of them were attacking me at once. They flew into my ear canal and all over my face. I musta slapped myself a hundred times.

Shemar slowly made his way to the boat. The water was already up to his neck. He used the paddle as a sort of flotation device. "Stay wit' me, JaMichael."

Oh, I was. Now that we were in the water there was no turning back. "Why the fuck would somebody park a boat in the middle of the water when it's filled with Alligators?"

"Just to see how serious you are about all of this shit!"

The water was too deep to walk now. We had to put the paddles in front of us and kick our legs. The water splashed all around. One by one the alligators dropped beneath it. My heart started beating so fast I kept forgetting to breathe.

"Where the fuck them alligators go?"

"Shit, we better hurry up." Shemar started kicking up the water all in my face. He made me panic because not only couldn't I breathe, I couldn't see either. "Come on, Ja-Michael!"

I felt something rough brush my hip, then something else knocked me hard on the thigh. "Arrgh!" I screamed I couldn't help it, I was freaking out.

"Did they bite you? What they bite off!" he hollered.

Now I was panicking, I didn't know where the Alligators were, but they were finna get me. I started kicking my legs like my life depended on it. I beat Shemar to the boat and jumped inside it first. He wasn't that far behind. He reached not seconds later, I pulled him up and into it. The boat had been tied to a buoy.

He laid flat on his back. "Damn, and to think we gotta do that shit again when we go back."

***

After paddling the boat across the creek, we came to a long tunnel. Shemar directed the boat to pull to the side of the tunnel. He stood up, wrapped a rope around a big metal hook and jumped off it, onto a platform. "Come on, JaMichael, we here."

As soon as he said those words two men in Cowboy hats and tight jeans stepped from the shadows with shotguns in their hands and half of their faces covered with masks.

"Let's go, Jefe' Pablo is waiting on you."

Both of us were snatched up and taken into the tunnel where we were placed on the back of four-wheelers.

Chapter 20

Jefe' Pablo stood five-feet-three inches tall. He had a red face and a big nose. Behind him were about thirty men. All of them were dressed in cowboy-like attire. They had on tight Levis' with big belt buckles. They wore button-up shirts that were tucked into their pants and Cowboy hats. I felt so uncomfortable. Each man was armed and appeared ready for action. We were in a cave-like atmosphere. It was rock and gravel all around. The walls had burning oil lamps around them. It had to be about fifty of them. I could even smell the strong stench of the burning oil. There were a number of bats that flew around overhead. I was trying my best not to focus on that fact because I didn't like bats, or nothing that resembled a rat, especially not a flying one.

Jefe' Pablo had both me and Shemar sit in a chair in front of him. He stood in front of Shemar and smoked a cigar. His big bushy mustache made him look sinister. "So, dis is da one to replace my black operation in Tennessee? You sure bout dis?" he asked, in broken English.

Shemar nodded. "He's certified, he comes from Royal blood."

"Royal blood, what does dat mean?" Jefe' Pablo inquired.

"Dat means his bloodline is full of Street Kings and King Pins. His father was the great, Taurus. So, it's in him to be a boss. I personally recommend, my lil' homie."

"Taurus, huh, dat the one all up in Russia and shit?"

"The one and only," Shemar said wit' pride.

Jefe' Pablo nodded. "You swear on your life for his qualifications?"

Shemar looked over at me. "I do."

Jefe' Pablo, looked him over for a long time, then he extended his hand, and shook Shemar's after he made him stand up. "In this game of death, all we have is our word. I'ma hold you to yours and put our blood on his qualifications. You officially have Texas, and this JaMichael here will have Tennessee. Mikey's out and he is in." He sidestepped and held his hand out to me.

I stood up and shook it, it felt rough, almost scaly. "Thank you, Jefe' Pablo."

"Don't thank me, thank Shemar. His life rides on your success, with your own of course." He shook my hand and pulled his back. "A'ight then, it's settled. JaMichael, you got two weeks to breathe. After that, somebody will reach out to you with instructions. Shemar you will be his point man, and all will go smooth. There is a lot of money to be made and we're going to make it. I'll see you gentlemen at a later juncture. Vamanos!" he hollered. His men closed in, then escorted us out of his one of many hideouts.

***

After our long travel through the swamp, and another close call with a few Alligators, we were back in the truck smelling funky as hell. Shemar pulled away and turned down the music that was at first blaring out of his speakers. "How you feel lil' homie?"

I moved my toes around in my shoes. They were wet, and I was itching all over. On top of that, we were both smelling real foul. I couldn't wait to get in the shower and get clean. "I feel like I'm ready to see my sister, I miss, Jahliya. Let's go and make this shit happen."

"Nigga we on our way, Houston here we come. I know you been waiting a long time, and that baby girl done been through hell. I hope that everything turns out for the best." We were both silent for a long time after he said that.

I was lost in deep thought and praying for the best. It had been too long of a journey for things to not turn out the way they were supposed to. I didn't think Jehovah hated our bloodline that much, that he would give us a bad ending. Our lives had been tragic enough. He got onto the freeway after much traveling through the woods. He grabbed a towel from his glove compartment and handed it to me, then he grabbed one for himself. As we rolled down the highway the sun was just coming up. It looked like a big red fireball, and like we were going to drive right into it.

"Shemar, what made you vouch for me with your life? You don't even know me like that?"

Shemar smiled and looked over at me. "I see a whole lot of me in you, lil' homie. I can tell you are meant to be a boss in every sense of the word. On top of that, I know who yo' daddy is. Your Pops is a good dude. He bred by the slums fa real, and he was one of the first kingpins that really put me in the game. I owe him, straight up."

"Them Cartel boys seem real serious. You telling me that if I make a mistake that we all die?"

"Yep, that's the way it goes. They don't do mistakes, and they don't do excuses. You fuck up once, they get rid of you. That's the way they are, it's how they have become one of the deadliest entities in the world."

"What about school and the books I wanna write? What about my movies?"

"You can do all of that, as long as you handle their bidness first. They allow you to live your life, it's just on their terms. It's gone be a while before they let you show yo' face to promote yo' shit, too. You're about to be too important in the South lil' Bruh. It's fucked up but that's just the way it is. You wanna know something?"

"What's that?"

"I always wanted to be a rapper growing up, and I was a beast wit' it too, but after I got mingled in with these Cartel niggas all that shit went out the window because I couldn't promote my shit. In order to have longevity as a kingpin, you must stay in the shadows, not just to avoid the Feds, but to keep your life. If it seems you are bringing heat to their infrastructures, they will annihilate you, and your entire family tree."

"What?"

He nodded. "This shit is serious. Fuck that fake shit that you see in the movies and fuck them false ass hood novels. Nall, this is real life shit. You gotta be on point, or you will become the target, trust that." He scratched his head. "But don't get me wrong it ain't all bad. You about to live real good. Money will never be an object, and you are about to meet some of the baddest bitches in the universe. Nigga, if you play yo' cards right you might even hob knob with the right ma'fuckas that's really got that cake and get you some Alien pussy."

"Some what?"

"Ah, you thought they wasn't real. A'ight, you finna see shit that blows yo mind. Money is the true King of the universe, not man."

I couldn't do nothing but shake my head. "So, what did you do about your dreams? Don't it kill you, that you was never able to be a rapper?"

"Not no more. I still write music and all my artists are in the top five of the game. I'm talking literally one through five. Behind the scenes is where the money is anyway. You got a lot to learn. Come on, we finna switch whips and get clean so we can go buss this nigga's brain."

***

We didn't make it to the fifth Ward in Houston until later that night, at around eleven o'clock. We pulled into the alley right behind Liberty Street. Nicki was already parked to the side in a black on black Chevy Caprice Classic. When she saw our van, she jumped out of her whip, jogged back to the van, and climbed in the side door, sliding it close behind her.

"A'ight, look, I got two of my girls in there with Mikey, right now. They been going back and forth to the bathroom all night sending me texts and keeping me updated. They say he in there fucked up. He been sipping Lean and tooting that Mexican Tar. It should be a piece of cake, but we gotta move. Even though the Cartel done lifted their security from him, he still got loyal followers from Orange Mound that's supposed to be on their way down here. Also, Liberty jumping right now, all the fiends are out chasing a fix, so here." She handed me a Glock with a silencer on it. "When you done, those Hittas, right there gon' wrap his ass up in plastic and call it a day. He going to the hogs."

Shemar laughed at that. "Know that."

Nicki kissed my cheek. "Y'all get in there. Good luck boo." She climbed back out of the van and closed it back.

I pulled my mask down and tucked her Glock on my hip. "Let's do this big homie."

Shemar nodded. "A'ight, let's go."

I looked out the window, Nicki was already at the back door, waving me over. I jumped out of the van and took off across the backyard. I was beside her in seconds. She moved out of the way and I stepped into the hallway. I could smell the stench of piss, and crack cocaine, it was strong. Baby rats were crawling all over the floor and there were holes in the steps leading to the backdoor that was already wide open.

Before I could make my way up them two females appeared. They saw me and froze.

Nicki put a finger to her lips to shush them. She waved for them to leave out the back door. They followed her commands. Shemar appeared, at my side, then I took the holey stairs two at a time with my pistol out. The backdoor led into a hallway, I rushed inside. My heart was beating harder than I ever remember. I went past one bedroom, then two, then the bathroom. When I made it to the living room Mikey was just lowering his head to take up a line of Tar. He placed the hundred-dollar bill inside one of his nostrils, but before he could inhale I grabbed him by the hair and slammed his face so hard into the glass table that it shattered. He fell face first. The bottles of Moët landed on top of him.

"Where the fuck is, Jahliya?" I snapped pulling him up by the hair and slinging him against the wall.

His back hit it hard. He slid down it and closed his eyes for a second. When he opened them and saw my face they got big. "Shit!" He reached under his shirt to go for his gun.

Shemar kicked it out of his hand and moved out of the way. "Fuck nigga, ain't gon' be none of that."

I jumped on him and started hitting him as hard as I could, and as fast as I could with my gun laying on the side of him. After two minutes of this, he started hollering.

"She downstairs locked in the room—she downstairs! Get the fuck off me! It ain't my fault, it's his!" He pointed at Shemar.

Shemar kicked him in the chest and proceeded to stomp him out. "Where she at nigga?"

Mikey wiped the blood from his face. "She downstairs, chained up in the room."

I snatched him up. "Nigga come on, you finna take me to her."

I forced him into the basement and threw him down the last four steps. He fell to the floor and jumped up. He rushed to the back of the basement and pointed at the locked room. There was a big door with a Master lock on the outside of it. He went into his pocket and came out with a key.

"You a dirty nigga, Shemar. You got this nigga thinking I did this shit when you, and his—"

Boom! Boom! Boom!

Mikey flew into the door with the back of his head knocked off. He fell sideways and slumped lifeless on the ground with his eyes wide open.

"Fuck that nigga, JaMichael." He stomped him and picked up the key.

"Why you kill him? What if she ain't in here? What the fuck?"

Shemar ignored me. He jiggled the key into the lock, and it clicked. He took it off and slammed it to the floor. It ricocheted and bounced up.

I moved him out of the way and tried to open the door. It appeared stuck. I took one step back and kicked that bitch in with all my might. As soon as it opened, I rushed inside!

To Be Continued...
Heartless Goon 4
Coming Soon

Submission Guideline

Submit the first three chapters of your completed manuscript to ldpsubmissions@gmail.com, subject line: Your book's title. The manuscript must be in a .doc file and sent as an attachment. Document should be in Times New Roman, double spaced and in size 12 font. Also, provide your synopsis and full contact information. If sending multiple submissions, they must each be in a separate email.

Have a story but no way to send it electronically? You can still submit to LDP/Ca$h Presents. Send in the first three chapters, written or typed, of your completed manuscript to:

LDP: Submissions Dept
Po Box 870494
Mesquite, Tx 75187

DO NOT send original manuscript. Must be a duplicate.

Provide your synopsis and a cover letter containing your full contact information.

Thanks for considering LDP and Ca$h Presents.

Coming Soon from Lock Down Publications/Ca$h Presents

BOW DOWN TO MY GANGSTA

By **Ca$h**

TORN BETWEEN TWO

By **Coffee**

BLOOD STAINS OF A SHOTTA **III**

By **Jamaica**

STEADY MOBBIN **III**

By **Marcellus Allen**

BLOOD OF A BOSS **VI**

SHADOWS OF THE GAME II

By **Askari**

LOYAL TO THE GAME **IV**

By **T.J. & Jelissa**

A DOPEBOY'S PRAYER **II**

By **Eddie "Wolf" Lee**

IF LOVING YOU IS WRONG... **III**

By **Jelissa**

TRUE SAVAGE **VII**

MIDNIGHT CARTEL

DOPE BOY MAGIC II

By **Chris Green**

BLAST FOR ME **III**

DUFFLE BAG CARTEL **IV**

HEARTLESS GOON **IV**

A SAVAGE DOPEBOY II

DRUG LORDS II

By **Ghost**

A HUSTLER'S DECEIT III

KILL ZONE **II**

BAE BELONGS TO ME III

SOUL OF A MONSTER III

By **Aryanna**

THE COST OF LOYALTY **III**

By **Kweli**

THE SAVAGE LIFE III

By **J-Blunt**

KING OF NEW YORK V

COKE KINGS IV

BORN HEARTLESS III

By **T.J. Edwards**

GORILLAZ IN THE BAY V

De'Kari

THE STREETS ARE CALLING II

Duquie Wilson

KINGPIN KILLAZ IV

STREET KINGS III

PAID IN BLOOD III

CARTEL KILLAZ III

Hood Rich

SINS OF A HUSTLA II

ASAD

TRIGGADALE III

Elijah R. Freeman

KINGZ OF THE GAME V

Playa Ray

SLAUGHTER GANG IV

RUTHLESS HEART II

By Willie Slaughter

THE HEART OF A SAVAGE II

By Jibril Williams

FUK SHYT II

By Blakk Diamond

THE DOPEMAN'S BODYGAURD II

By Tranay Adams

TRAP GOD II

By Troublesome

YAYO II

A SHOOTER'S AMBITION II

By S. Allen

GHOST MOB

Stilloan Robinson

KINGPIN DREAMS

By Paper Boi Rari

CREAM

By Yolanda Moore

SON OF A DOPE FIEND II

By Renta

FOREVER GANGSTA II

By Adrian Dulan

LOYALTY AIN'T PROMISED
By Keith Williams
THE PRICE YOU PAY FOR LOVE
By Destiny Skai
THE LIFE OF A HOOD STAR
By Rashia Wilson
TOE TAGZ II
By Ah'Million

<u>Available Now</u>

RESTRAINING ORDER **I & II**
By **CA$H & Coffee**
LOVE KNOWS NO BOUNDARIES **I II & III**
By **Coffee**
RAISED AS A GOON I, II, III & IV
BRED BY THE SLUMS I, II, III
BLAST FOR ME I & II
ROTTEN TO THE CORE I II III
A BRONX TALE I, II, III
DUFFEL BAG CARTEL I II III
HEARTLESS GOON
A SAVAGE DOPEBOY
HEARTLESS GOON I II III
DRUG LORDS
By **Ghost**
LAY IT DOWN **I & II**

LAST OF A DYING BREED

BLOOD STAINS OF A SHOTTA I & II

By **Jamaica**

LOYAL TO THE GAME

LOYAL TO THE GAME II

LOYAL TO THE GAME III

LIFE OF SIN I, II III

By **TJ & Jelissa**

BLOODY COMMAS I & II

SKI MASK CARTEL I II & III

KING OF NEW YORK I II,III IV

RISE TO POWER I II III

COKE KINGS I II III

BORN HEARTLESS I II

By **T.J. Edwards**

IF LOVING HIM IS WRONG…I & II

LOVE ME EVEN WHEN IT HURTS I II III

By **Jelissa**

WHEN THE STREETS CLAP BACK I & II III

By **Jibril Williams**

A DISTINGUISHED THUG STOLE MY HEART I II & III

LOVE SHOULDN'T HURT I II III IV

RENEGADE BOYS I II III IV

By **Meesha**

A GANGSTER'S CODE I &, II III

A GANGSTER'S SYN I II III

THE SAVAGE LIFE I II

Ghost

By J-Blunt

PUSH IT TO THE LIMIT

By **Bre' Hayes**

BLOOD OF A BOSS **I, II, III, IV, V**

SHADOWS OF THE GAME

By **Askari**

THE STREETS BLEED MURDER **I, II & III**

THE HEART OF A GANGSTA I II& III

By **Jerry Jackson**

CUM FOR ME

CUM FOR ME 2

CUM FOR ME 3

CUM FOR ME 4

CUM FOR ME 5

An **LDP Erotica Collaboration**

BRIDE OF A HUSTLA **I II & II**

THE FETTI GIRLS **I, II& III**

CORRUPTED BY A GANGSTA I, II III, IV

BLINDED BY HIS LOVE

By **Destiny Skai**

WHEN A GOOD GIRL GOES BAD

By **Adrienne**

THE COST OF LOYALTY I II

By Kweli

A GANGSTER'S REVENGE **I II III & IV**

THE BOSS MAN'S DAUGHTERS

THE BOSS MAN'S DAUGHTERS II

THE BOSSMAN'S DAUGHTERS III

THE BOSSMAN'S DAUGHTERS IV

THE BOSS MAN'S DAUGHTERS **V**

A SAVAGE LOVE **I & II**

BAE BELONGS TO ME I II

A HUSTLER'S DECEIT I, II, III

WHAT BAD BITCHES DO I, II, III

SOUL OF A MONSTER I II

KILL ZONE

By **Aryanna**

A KINGPIN'S AMBITON

A KINGPIN'S AMBITION **II**

I MURDER FOR THE DOUGH

By **Ambitious**

TRUE SAVAGE

TRUE SAVAGE II

TRUE SAVAGE **III**

TRUE SAVAGE **IV**

TRUE SAVAGE **V**

TRUE SAVAGE **VI**

DOPE BOY MAGIC

By **Chris Green**

A DOPEBOY'S PRAYER

By **Eddie "Wolf" Lee**

THE KING CARTEL **I, II & III**

By **Frank Gresham**

THESE NIGGAS AIN'T LOYAL **I, II & III**

Ghost

By **Nikki Tee**

GANGSTA SHYT **I II &III**

By **CATO**

THE ULTIMATE BETRAYAL

By **Phoenix**

BOSS'N UP **I , II & III**

By **Royal Nicole**

I LOVE YOU TO DEATH

By Destiny J

I RIDE FOR MY HITTA

I STILL RIDE FOR MY HITTA

By **Misty Holt**

LOVE & CHASIN' PAPER

By **Qay Crockett**

TO DIE IN VAIN

SINS OF A HUSTLA

By **ASAD**

BROOKLYN HUSTLAZ

By **Boogsy Morina**

BROOKLYN ON LOCK I & II

By **Sonovia**

GANGSTA CITY

By **Teddy Duke**

A DRUG KING AND HIS DIAMOND I & II III

A DOPEMAN'S RICHES

HER MAN, MINE'S TOO I, II

CASH MONEY HO'S

By Nicole Goosby
TRAPHOUSE KING **I II & III**
KINGPIN KILLAZ I II III
STREET KINGS I II
PAID IN BLOOD **I II**
CARTEL KILLAZ I II
By **Hood Rich**
LIPSTICK KILLAH **I, II, III**
CRIME OF PASSION I II & III
By **Mimi**
STEADY MOBBN' **I, II, III**
By **Marcellus Allen**
WHO SHOT YA **I, II, III**
SON OF A DOPE FIEND
Renta
GORILLAZ IN THE BAY **I II III IV**
DE'KARI
TRIGGADALE I II
Elijah R. Freeman
GOD BLESS THE TRAPPERS I, II, III
THESE SCANDALOUS STREETS I, II, III
FEAR MY GANGSTA I, II, III
THESE STREETS DON'T LOVE NOBODY I, II
BURY ME A G I, II, III, IV, V
A GANGSTA'S EMPIRE I, II, III, IV
THE DOPEMAN'S BODYGAURD
Tranay Adams

THE STREETS ARE CALLING

Duquie Wilson

MARRIED TO A BOSS... I II III

By Destiny Skai & Chris Green

KINGZ OF THE GAME I II III IV

Playa Ray

SLAUGHTER GANG I II III

RUTHLESS HEART

By Willie Slaughter

THE HEART OF A SAVAGE

By Jibril Williams

FUK SHYT

By Blakk Diamond

DON'T F#CK WITH MY HEART I II

By Linnea

ADDICTED TO THE DRAMA I II III

By Jamila

YAYO

A SHOOTER'S AMBITION

By S. Allen

TRAP GOD

By Troublesome

FOREVER GANGSTA

By Adrian Dulan

TOE TAGZ

By Ah'Million

BOOKS BY LDP'S CEO, CA$H

TRUST IN NO MAN

TRUST IN NO MAN 2

TRUST IN NO MAN 3

BONDED BY BLOOD

SHORTY GOT A THUG

THUGS CRY

THUGS CRY 2

THUGS CRY 3

TRUST NO BITCH

TRUST NO BITCH 2

TRUST NO BITCH 3

TIL MY CASKET DROPS

RESTRAINING ORDER

RESTRAINING ORDER 2

IN LOVE WITH A CONVICT

Coming Soon

BONDED BY BLOOD 2

BOW DOWN TO MY GANGSTA

Ghost

Printed in the USA
CPSIA information can be obtained
at www.ICGtesting.com
LVHW021143251123
764902LV00063B/3472